CARINA

CARINA

The Yacht that Refused to Die

Valerie Langrish Warner

Book Guild Publishing
Sussex, England

First published in Great Britain in 2010 by
The Book Guild
Pavilion View
19 New Road
Brighton, BN1 1UF

While the main characters in this book were real people,
this is a work of fiction.

Typesetting in Baskerville by
Keyboard Services, Luton, Bedfordshire

Printed in Great Britain by
CPI Antony Rowe

A catalogue record for this book is available from
The British Library

ISBN 978 1 84624 413 1

Author's Note

This book is based on the extraordinary history of the Motor Yacht *Karin II* built for Hermann Goëring in 1937 and still afloat today.

However, the story outlined and the characters depicted are a mixture of recorded events and the writer's experiences and imagination.

Prologue

The midday heat of this January day was far hotter than any of the farmers, working the rich fields surrounding Christchurch, had ever known. Some returned their tractors to their barns for shade, some decided not to venture further than their yards, as they felt the hot circulating gusts of wind that often presaged a lightning storm.

In Lavender Farm Cottage, Jess, the farmer's wife, was busy preparing one of her own hens for the cooking pot. The plan was for a celebration supper that evening. It was fifty years since she had married Tomas and they had emigrated to New Zealand to set up a lavender farm. Her brother, his wife and their unmarried daughter had recently flown from the United States to stay with them for a month. It was their first visit and they were looking forward to travelling around South Island in a rented motor home to explore the mountain village of Hanmer where they would bathe in the hot springs and play golf. All three were avid golfers and knew that the island had many clubs where visitors were trusted to put their dues in a box, and just play. They planned to drive north to Nelson and spend a few days wandering the islands and beaches around Picton. The lakes near Mount Cook and further south near Queenstown were to be explored fully before they returned along the east coast route through Dunedin and Timaru, stopping to play golf on picturesque courses. She knew that they would love Christchurch as much as she did with its English-style river gardens, modern shopping areas and well-preserved churches and colleges. She would let them catch up on some sleep so they would have all the energy they would need for their tour, starting the next day. She would love to travel with them but she had work to do cutting and preparing the lavender heads for making health oils.

She turned on the overhead light in the kitchen; it was very dark and quiet outside. Oh heavens, she thought, we are in for quite a downpour. She worried that their bushes were not adequately protected and called for her husband to check that the greenhouse doors were closed. There was a loud clap of thunder, followed by one even louder, and streak after streak of fork lightning illuminated the windows. The electrical storm was directly overhead and it sounded as if their world was cracking apart; exploding into many pieces as if stun-bombed. It will soon blow over, she thought. The storm did not move away, but stayed threateningly above their cottage. The regular explosions gained in strength. The lamp went out and she fumbled for matches to light the table candles. Hearing shouts from the bedroom above she started to climb the stairs to reassure her relatives.

At that exact moment the neatly piled logs that the farmer had painstakingly chopped for their winter fires, were set alight. The bone-dry wood, with jutting sawn branches still gripping dead leaves, flamed instantly. The heat from the fire caused the large Calor gas tank behind the cedar shed to explode. The farmer was killed instantly; his body shooting upwards and landing on the raging pile of wood. In panic, his wife ran to check the upstairs windows but also found the cottage enveloped in flames. It was too late for them to jump down. The windows of the kitchen had blown out and within minutes the downstairs was on fire. Flames had devoured the pine staircase and the wooden framed cottage was a tinderbox.

Because of the time difference between Florida and

Christchurch it was twenty-four hours before her son Alex picked up the phone to talk to his parents and sister about their flight and first impressions of New Zealand. There was no ringing tone and no answer. He rang again an hour later and kept trying – listening to the same eerie static-filled silence. His pulse was racing, his heart thumping in his chest and his brow bathed in beads of sweat when he at last admitted to himself that there was something very wrong, and asked the overseas telephone operator for the number of the Christchurch Police Station.

He was passed from officer to clerk and back again to an officer before someone had the guts to tell him the news. An inferno had devastated Lavender Cottage and seven acres of lavender plantings, barns, stables, sheds and the owners – his uncle and aunt. Their visitors, his parents and sister had been found an hour later by the fifty firemen who doused the flames. There was nothing left of them but charred remains, and these would be returned to him in the United States – if that was what he wanted. He certainly had no intention of visiting the blackened ruins; so agreed.

One

An early evening sea fret rolled in from the Intracoastal Waterway, Anastasia Island and the Atlantic Ocean beyond, which partially obscured the Castillo de San Marcos, the national monument in Florida. Alex tried to avoid ruminating over the loss of his family five years previously. Instead he smiled to himself and remembered something less harrowing: how he had struggled to describe this monument for a tour brochure: one of many small assignments he accepted to fill in the empty spaces between writing and printing by searching for a new project.

Starting to jog along the river path he overtook several groups of visitors, speaking in other languages, and wondered if they could have read his piece before taking 'the tour'. Would they know that this ancient building at the point was constructed of coquina rock in the 1600s to protect the citizens of St Augustine and the Spanish ships laden with treasures? He had written that this dark monster, thirty-three feet high with walls sixteen feet wide at their base, was the oldest and largest masonry fort in the United States. It had created a safe haven for the development of the Spanish city behind; a place which he had called home for all of his life. It was one area on the south-east coast that had been bypassed by hurricanes – so far. As he passed by he touched the damp scarred stone for luck – something that had been in short supply.

The cathedral clock chimed six o'clock. He slowed to a walk after crossing Castillo Drive, past the new multi-storey car park and the parallel line of coaches behind, and made his way through the old narrow streets of the Colonial Spanish Quarter. The main trouble with exercise, he thought, was the thirst that followed. His son, Jake, was a keep-fit freak. As, for that matter was his wife, Mary. Both stressed that 'middle-aged' desk-bound men developed beer paunches and needed regular visits to the gym and daily walks in order to stay slim. He looked down to check – then turned sideways to view his body profile in a shop window. So far, so good. Maybe a small beer would do no harm, but he must be home before 6.30 p.m. On Saturday night he was on barbecue duty. As he walked into the Bay Inn he debated with himself over the choice of marinade for the chicken and dressing for the salad. Cooking – what a hobby!

'Well now, look who's here,' was his welcome from the bright-eyed half-Irish girl behind the bar counter. 'It's a while since you stopped by. Not with Mary?'

'Hi, Ellen. No, she visits her Mom every Saturday afternoon, at the Oaks Retirement Community. It was her Mom's own decision – to be with her friends.'

Having paid, he took his frosted glass to an outside table, not wanting a long chat with the barmaid – a terrible gossip – only to catch sight of a couple of friends sitting in the corner, leaning back against the brightly painted wall. He had known Brian and Don, who own and run Plantation Travel, since their school days, and often read of faraway places in their holiday brochures. Being one of many Americans who have never left home shores, Alex only enjoyed travel vicariously. He knew, however, that he should make more of an effort to learn about the rest of the world, as it could only help his writing. This subject was something of a joke amongst his friends, who made a point of showing him their holiday photos and videos whenever possible. He would love to visit Europe, Africa, Russia or China but had never had the means. Savings for the summer break had only stretched as far as holidays on his home turf; so often when he wrote articles or stories he either gleaned information from the library or from the web. He thanked the Lord that he had a great imagination.

'Alex, come and join us,' Brian called. 'We've just been to an agents' conference and may have something of interest for you.'

Alex pulled up a third chair and sat down, crossed his long legs and sipped his beer.

'Not one of your jokes, I hope.'

'Hear what we have to tell you, and then decide,' said Don. 'We won a holiday prize for two in Paris, which neither of us can take. We have been wondering if this could be your big adventure.'

'You are joking?'

'But wait … there is more, as the ads always tell us. There is a holiday sponsorship deal to a developing resort in, of all places, Egypt. Apparently several hotel chains need to boost their tourism figures after a downturn following 9/11 and part of the recent "Accord Agreement" was to send "stabilizing funds" to that part of the world.'

Alex was quiet for a while, considering this unusual idea, before he answered,

'Hey, that sounds great, but however much would it cost?

Alex knew that if he was to go on this adventure he would have to take Mary and Jake with him, and that Jake would love the chance to tour the Pyramids and the Sphinx. Jake had been keen on Egyptian history since they had visited the Tutankhamen Exhibition in LA. That must be over three years ago, he thought. He was fourteen then and had had ideas of becoming an archaeologist ever since.

'Look,' Don replied. 'Before we go any further let us

work out an itinerary and the expenses for you and we will talk again. Maybe you would like to find out if Mary and Jake are keen and, if so, when you would like to go.'

'It would have to be during the summer break. Is that possible?'

'I believe the weather varies very little in those parts. I'll look into it,' promised Brian.

After glancing at his watch, and checking again with his friends if this was for real, Alex told them that he must get home to light the barbecue, and would talk later. He needed time to think things through before getting too involved. He walked slowly home – the long way. He ambled through the cloisters of the Litner Museum, pausing for a moment of reflection by the lily pond, which was once the swimming pool of the old Alcazar Hotel, built in 1888.

The seagulls shrieked their warning in time with the chimes of the city and should have been subtle reminders; but he was lost in a dream world as he brushed past some hanging ivy. Since the loss of his sister, with whom he had been close, and his energetic and loving parents, Alex had found himself dreaming a good deal of the time. He was yet to complete the mourning process – it had all happened so far away and so quickly. Talking to his parents in his head was a daily activity. How he missed the long discussions his family had enjoyed, whenever anyone had a problem or a special interest. Mary thought he was prone to dwell on his past and should start making more of an effort to work things out in the 'here and now'.

Mary made her third circuit of the many clocks at home that ticked her life away. There were at least two in every room, all telling a slightly different time; most inherited from her long-gone father. Whichever way she turned she was reminded that Alex was over an hour late.

This meant there was no supper in progress and she was both hungry and angry. Maybe, she thought, this was because she was very tired. Tired of her depressing weekly visits to see her mother, of her boring typing job, her over-active son, her … no she must not allow herself even to go there. After twenty-five years of marriage to a writer (who seemed to do very little writing) she was in a rut. He had been promising this 'bestseller' for donkey's years, and still his fees from freelancing and ghosting only brought in dribs and drabs. She was the mainstay of the family finances; she had been for years. At least Jake now ran his own sideline for pocket money. His latest brainwave – Jake's Dog Jog – was a dog-walking scheme that was really catching on amongst overloaded families and old dears who could not manage to walk their four-legged friends on a regular basis.

Stopping by the hall table, to sort through the mail once more, she studied her image in the mirror hanging above. She smoothed over the frown lines spreading across her forehead, checked out her still-white teeth, and drew fingers through her darkened bob. The stresses of the years were beginning to tell on her once-attractive looks. What could she do? She had been thinking of renting out two of their unused rooms to students, but dismissed the idea as impractical. It would only be possible if Alex was not at home. But could she face the full impact of this proposition? The idea screamed the stigma of a 'single parent family'.

The welcome sounds of a bicycle banging against the wooden sidings, the heavy tread of large feet and the banging of the front door screen brought Mary back to earth. At least one member of the family was home.

'What are you doing in the semi-dark, Mom?' Jake asked

as he dropped his bag and came over to hug her. Giving her a searching look he asked if she was OK and where his Dad had got to.

'I'm fine, just about to turn on the lights. Could you see to the barbecue for me? It seems Dad has forgotten or been delayed somewhere. I must make sure that I don't nag when he does arrive; not easy as I do feel really uptight.'

Jake laughed and teased her. 'I thought so. You have been having a go at both of us lately. Relax Mom, it's not so bad. Cool it ... I will pour you a glass of wine and we can listen to some music while we wait to see what happens. How was Gran?'

'She asked after you; when will you visit? She is still very alert; but she does go on so about the past. I hear the same memories every week.'

'I'll pop in on Wednesday – my half day – and try to remind her of other stories. How we constructed make-believe planes with her fire utensils and carpet cleaning pipes whenever we had a sleep-over ... oh good, here is Dad.'

Thinking that he could be in trouble Alex smiled defensively as he entered the hall, and apologized as he removed his trainers, dropping them in the basket.

'I'm rather late, sorry, but...'

Mary could not contain herself. 'You promised to have everything ready. You know damned well how tired I am on Saturday evenings, after a long week at work and all the chores at home, and visiting mother...' and she paused for breath.

'Yes, yes, but...'

'I don't want to hear your excuses! What have you done all day? Nothing. I just can't cope with everything. I am up to here,' she shouted, lifting her hand over the top of her head and running upstairs. Jake and Alex looked at each other and shrugged.

'What do you think about us cooking a wonderful supper and letting the delicious aroma entice her down?' Jake asked.

'Good idea, let's get to it,' agreed his father, entering the kitchen and reaching for his favourite cookery book. 'Let me see; how about Hawaiian Special? Read out the ingredients and I'll try to find them.'

Together they prepared a tempting glaze using crushed pineapple, brown sugar, lemon juice and mustard. Then they brushed both sides of two halved chickens, before plating them and placing them in the fridge to infuse. Next Alex lit the charcoal in their simple round barbecue. Anxious to take every precaution he turned down the draught control and adjusted the rack. They found and chopped lettuce, cucumber, olives, nuts, tomatoes and radishes, then mixed a raspberry vinegar, garlic and olive oil dressing. They tossed this on the salad. When the coals were glowing the chicken was arranged bone down, to be flipped after twenty minutes.

Soon the charcoal and sweet-tart fruity smells filled the still-misty air of the yard. Alex suggested that he would try to make amends with Mary if Jake collected the cutlery and plates and brought down a basket of bread.

'We are so lucky to be able to eat al fresco in February, even on a cool damp evening. Have you seen the photos of snow cover almost everywhere else? The thermometer reads sixty-two degrees; not bad if we wear our sweatshirts. Oh … thanks Jake for your help. We make a good team.'

He climbed the curving polished stairway to find their bedroom door locked. He called to Mary, 'Supper will be ready soon. Come down, I have something to talk to you about. Something we must share with Jake.'

When Mary appeared, she was a little bleary eyed but over her temper. Alex apologized again and asked if he could now tell them the reason why he had been late.

Uninterrupted this time he was able to replay for them his holiday discussion with Brian and Don, and watch their surprised expressions.

'If you really think that we can travel that far from home, you are mistaken,' Mary told him. 'Anyhow I have no desire to go to the Middle East ... Europe is another question altogether; but we just don't have the money.'

'Hold on a minute, Mary, I haven't finished; I may be paid for writing about our travels and advertisements in the resort. Jake would be able to help with this.'

Jake was obviously keen. He brushed his dark fringe out of his smiling eyes. His cheeks were flushed. 'You two both know that I find the whole Pharaoh scene mind-blowing. Remember King Tut, living in the 1350s BC, was not much older than I am now and was married and extremely wealthy. I have always wanted to visit Egypt and as for Paris ... well!'

'Hey, nothing is – to use what must have been an old Egyptian saying – carved in stone. I will have to go through the whole plan with the boys once we have discussed dates. Are you saying that you don't like the idea, Mary?'

'I'd just like to reserve judgement until I've heard all the details,' Mary replied. 'How long would we be away? I don't believe I could leave Mom for very long.'

Jake turned to her. 'Mom, if Dad can investigate further and make this scheme work, you could make your own arrangements to join us. Such chances only come once in a blue moon.'

'That's enough for now,' Alex told them. 'The chicken smells delicious. I vote that we eat before taking this any further. Come on through Mary.'

Taking his wife's hand he led her through onto the terrace.

It was not until the following weekend that Alex received Don's proposed itinerary and prices. The trip looked possible but they may need a small bank loan to cover the two nights in Paris for three. They would then fly to Cairo for a stop-over and on to Hurghada Airport, twenty kilometres south of El Gouna where they would spend ten days before flying home via Geneva, Switzerland. What a trip this was going to be. However, he must remember that he would be on a working holiday. Surely this would persuade Mary.

After telling Mary and Jake the news, and helping to clear away their supper dishes, he was surprised to hear that Mary had changed her mind. She would, after all, love to go; and had an idea.

'Why don't the three of us research one part of this adventure and share our information. This would enable us to be more prepared in these strange countries, and Dad could use our work for his writing. We have three months ahead of us: plenty of time.'

'I like it,' said Alex. 'I must take the resort of El Gouna as this is already my remit.'

'Yeah, and I will add to the research I have done on the civilizations of the Nile,' Jake added. 'This leaves you with Paris, Mom. How does that sound?'

'I'll visit the library tomorrow,' she replied, handing them both a mug of strong coffee.

Jake's first inclination was to dive for the atlas to establish the borders and topography of Egypt. He printed an enlargement of the country on the school library photocopier and posted it above his computer desk. With coloured pins he flagged the main cities and delineated the border and River Nile with felt tips. He had imagined the large desert tract, and was taken aback to see that Sudan in the south, Libya to the west, and Saudi Arabia to the east, were all approximately three times the size of Egypt. The Mediterranean Sea bordered the north of the country for over four hundred miles, with the Suez Canal on the north-east corner leading into the Red Sea.

His main areas of interest were the capital, Cairo, with the nearby pyramids of the Pharaohs, who lived more than 1,000 years before Tutankhamen; Luxor, about 300 miles south on the Nile, with the Valley of Kings on the opposite river bank; and Hurghada on the Red Sea three and a half hours by coach east of Luxor. It may be difficult to fit in a trip to the Aswan Dam this time – it was another two-and-a-half hours to the south.

Wanting to know more about the country and the people he brought home a pile of books. Lying on his duvet he tackled a detailed description by American writer Rosemary Mahoney of her solo rowing expedition from Aswan to Qena – 120 miles. From her extensive research and colourful details of the lives and beliefs of the people she encountered Jake began to understand the many differences between their lives and his. Some were distasteful and confusing. Feeling drowsy, he put down the book and pensively reviewed his overall impressions. Then, sitting bolt upright, he slapped his forehead. Shouting 'hell' he jumped off the bed and descended the stairs four at a time.

He found Mary busy sweeping the porch. 'Sit down a minute, Mom. I have just found out … we cannot go to Egypt in the summer.'

Mary sat and stared at her son. 'What on earth do you mean?' she asked in a tired voice.

'I have just been reading of a true adventure on the River Nile. The writer describes the almost unbearable heat – and that was in April. There is no way we could exist in mid-summer; besides everything closes for tourists, as it is the "off season". We will have to cancel. Why didn't Brian tell us?'

'I will ring Brian right away – Dad said he promised to check the climate – we may have to re-arrange the dates,' Mary decided and made for the study. She returned minutes later to tell Jake that everything was 'on hold' until Dad returned from the library. 'It's weird,' she said, 'brochures and tour books on Paris have mentioned the same thing. The city is empty in July as all the families spend the summer months by the sea, with their Dad joining them for weekends.'

Later, having heard their findings, Alex made a quick decision. 'If we can organize ourselves we can go during the April break. The holiday would only be two weeks but this is long enough. We may have to defer our trip to Paris and Cairo. Let's see what Brian can arrange for us.'

'I read that Cairo is a hectic city – noisy, dirty and dangerous. So we could just change planes. Let's see … we have almost five weeks before lift-off … plenty of time,' Jake enthused.

'It's easy for you to say,' was Mary's only comment.

As it turned out they had to fly both ways via Switzerland. Alex, who had no wish to travel anywhere that was very hot, promised a French holiday another time, if possible. This was a grave disappointment to Mary but she tried to put on a brave face as it was a setback for Jake also. He would be unable to explore the pyramids and tombs as hoped. Maybe not a bad thing, he thought, as he needed more time to read through the numerous chronicles written over the centuries in order to fully understand the country. 'Another time,' he promised himself.

To cheer them up Alex presented a portfolio of photos he had collected of El Gouna, and told them a little about the place. 'This town is new: completely different from the ancient cities you have been researching, Jake. There are guided excursions from there to the historical sites however. How does that sound? Apparently a man called Sawiris, who ran a hotel development group, got a number of his business friends to invest in this beautiful spot as a holiday retreat some twenty years ago. They have almost completed what they set out to do – carve a paradise from the desert. We'll find out.'

After a pause Jake told him, 'It is not really the modern Egypt that interests me, but from the look of things we can have a good holiday. They seem to have plenty of water sports and a great night life.'

Mary and Alex looked at each other and groaned. They knew how worried they always were when Jake was out at night. Over the years they talked with their friends and each other over the possible disadvantages of having an only child. Having experienced a difficult breach-birth with Jake, Mary never wanted another baby. She was an only child herself and, after her father had died young in a car accident, enjoyed a happy relationship with her mother; maturing early into a self-sufficient teenager. Alex, on the other hand, was one of four siblings and would have liked a large family. But he was very proud of Jake, who had always had many friends and hobbies and grown to be a well-adjusted young man. They never 'spoilt' him with toys and games and expensive holidays but took care to give him individual attention, a good home environment and the moral guidance they saw was lacking with some other children. Their major fear was that he would be led into trouble – drink, drugs or illegal pranks – by his peer group. So far Jake had been very motivated to succeed at school and with sports and had not shown any interest in associating with the rowdies. So Alex had set aside his early longings to have a daughter and concentrated his efforts on being a good dad to his intelligent son.

Soon however, he would be leaving for some far-flung university and only making occasional visits home. That would be a difficult time for Alex, who increasingly found his marriage to be lacking in companionship and fun. Maybe if I work on it, he thought, this holiday could change all that; a new start.

Two

As his parents slept off their exhaustion after two days of travel to Egypt, Jake rose early, dressed quickly, and slipped out of their suite. He planned to explore El Gouna as the sun rose, and to report on his findings at breakfast. He walked quietly through what the holiday publicity booklet had described as 'a stunningly spacious' reception hall of the Mövenpick Hotel. There was nobody around as he pushed through the double doors leading to the courtyard gardens beyond. He had not expected to be staying five-star Swiss style, on a bay, with all mod cons. They had air-conditioning, Internet connections and satellite television, for they were 'exclusive guests', whatever that meant. He hoped that his father had managed to organize a large discount.

As the sky changed to a deep yellow, turning the sea to gold, Jake scanned the horizon of the still Red Sea for signs of life. It was only six o'clock and the world was asleep. On the beach he found one camel standing and another sitting with their keeper sleeping nearby under a huge straw umbrella. They were the only occupants. In the distance he could see the modern yellow and the Roman red towers, minarets and arches of the town. The buildings were jumbled together like a childhood set of building bricks: all levels, heights and sizes. There was a temporary peace: no gabbling people, no repetitive birds, no jumping fish or yapping dogs. The only sounds were of the gently tinkling masts in the far marina. He knew that this would change very soon. This development had won many architectural awards and been dubbed 'the Venice of Egypt' but his first impression was of Toy Town.

He sat for a while on the sea wall as the sky brightened before jogging around the hotel grounds. He passed the clay tennis courts, the diving centre, the pools and spa; also the Seafood Restaurant and bar terraces. This was a classy place but with no rivers where did the fresh water come from? Another worry was how they would they be able to afford to eat at the hotel? The hotel was a mile or so from the nightlife: hopefully it would be safe to walk back late at night. With so many imponderables he couldn't wait for his folk to wake up.

A wizened old man in reception was about to go off duty as Jake passed the desk. He was rubbing his eyes and did not want to chat. He reluctantly passed Jake a list of 'Dine Around' Restaurants which would allow them to substitute any meal at their own hotel for a visit to other establishments – a great idea. He was also given an activity brochure for deep sea diving, sailing, water skiing, golfing or riding – all included. Even better! Jake asked him about their hire car. The old man reached behind for a set of hanging keys and dangled them in front of Jake's nose.

'Tell your father, his car is in the car park.'

'Thanks, I will,' said Jake as he strode for the lift, which opened as he arrived. Five young people emerged clutching diving gear and talking to each other in English. They took no notice of Jake, so he approached to find out who they were.

It turned out that he had met an experienced group of divers from an English scuba diving club. They travelled together every Easter. Jake said that he would love to join the group for the five days they had left of their holiday. He had brought his diving log book with him. They told him how they had been exploring the reefs around the lagoons; taking underwater photos of delicate coloured corals, shipwrecks and shoals of exotic fish. They were off to the beach breakfast bar. Jake promised to join them later.

Alex and Mary were delighted that Jake had made friends so quickly. They were now free to explore the resort at their leisure without worrying about his safety. They would arrange a two-day tour for Jake to the Valley of the Kings and Queen Hatshepsut's Temple next week. Alex imagined how lost Jake would feel when his new diving friends returned home.

While Mary enjoyed the sunshine, swam in the hot salty Red Sea and the pools, or took advantage of relaxing treatments in the Spa, Alex toured the resort on foot. He was unable to use his Volkswagen hire car in the traffic-free town but toured the surrounding area. He made notes for tour articles:

a. Rooms spacious, clean, wonderful views of lagoons. Linen changed and mini-bar restocked daily.
b. Refurbishing and building work on room 'clusters' still unfinished.
c. Service in hotels and restaurants quick, efficient, friendly and unobtrusive. Few table-to-table peddlers.
d. Apart from a few drunken tourists roaming the town in the evening, the resort is wonderfully peaceful with many sporting activities.
e. Perfect weather: hot sun, little wind, clear skies. No rain.
f. Every interest and comfort catered for.

Turning to tourist blogs on his computer he found a few overbooking problems. Some visitors had been taken to hotels other than the ones they had booked; a problem encountered worldwide.

'Oh, damn, damn, damn,' he cried and tore up the pages, depositing them in the large waste paper basket, just as Mary returned.

'What on earth is the matter with you?' she asked, as she hung her wet towel on the balcony.

'I have been trying to write something useful for hours. What I did write was just the sort of boring rubbish that is written about any hotel, anywhere, for the management. I must find some vivid descriptions, jazzy life stories and in-depth comparisons: some soul. This place was designed for top people and is attracting crowds of holiday makers on cheap tours. As it is so expensive to provide areas of green grass, distilled water, fresh food, equipment and labour in desert regions; this place can only go downhill in difficult financial times.

'So what do you want to do? You've been inside all day.'

'Let's walk down to the harbour now it's cooler and see if we can hire a speed boat for tomorrow. We can circumnavigate the town by water in the morning and take Jake water skiing in the afternoon. His friends are leaving early.'

'And your work?'

'Hey, something will turn up. This glossy brochure work is not my forte, as you know. Let's go.'

The Abu-Tig Marina was home for many types of craft: fishing trawlers, ketches, pristine motor yachts, catamarans and, in their shade, a small red motor boat with a 'for hire' notice on the windscreen. Alex approached a lad sitting on the wall, his knees bent next to his chin, and asked if he knew the owner.

'Yes sir, I am Mahmoud, the owner is my father. You want a ride in his boat? I will go for him.' He gathered up his white gallabiya in one hand and ran to the nearest building. His father spoke good English and was keen to negotiate a boat rental, but kept insisting that either he or his son should accompany them.

'I know the waters and reefs and will keep you safe,' he assured them.

'We have a boat like this in America,' Alex told him, 'and we will be quite safe. Show me the chart. We don't intend to venture far; just tour the lagoons.'

After studying the water depths on a creased worn chart, and some haggling over the cost, it was agreed that they could take the boat out by themselves in the morning for water skiing. In the evening the lad would join them for a tour of the town. His job would be to guard the boat while they visit the downtown Kafr, a sort of mall or market, and warn of any shallow waters, they were told. The arrangement was to meet at ten o'clock the following day to lend them water skis, life-jackets and a tow rope, and see them safely away from the dock.

The marina water was turning from pink to mauve and the sky was shaded from purple to pale coral as the sun sank below the horizon.

'Let's go back to the hotel and wait for Jake on the balcony,' Mary suggested. 'This is my favourite time. It's cool at last after the heat of the day and I love all the dim, exotic colours. The smells rising from the kitchen make me hungry.'

'Umm. I don't know Jake's plans, but maybe we can have supper together in the Sayadin Seafood Bar before he goes out. I expect his group will be having a farewell party later. We must warn him not to be too late as he must be up for skiing tomorrow.'

Despite a hangover from partaking of one too many of the 'Ten to Midnight' free drinks at the Horror Pub and dancing in the uproarious German Beergarten with his friends (the strobes vying with the moonlight), and walking home, Jake was awake by seven o'clock the next morning. He felt better after an early swim and found his parents up and dressed when he returned to the room. They were all keen to try the morning buffet by the pool; quicker than the service café.

'Wow, just what I need,' Jake said as he saw the array of goodies – cereals, fruits, pastries, sausages, eggs of all sorts, ham, beans and best of all the freshly baked bread.

As he selected his breakfast Alex recalled details of Egyptian agriculture problems. Cotton fields, once the mainstay of the country's economy – employing 28 per cent of the labour force and accounting for 20 per cent of exports – had been reduced as tourist numbers grew.

He looked at all the other tourists filling their plates and mouths. 'All these visitors must be eating most of the food produced locally,' he thought. There had been a downturn in tourism to Egypt after the Twin Towers disaster but grants and loans of more than $10 billion had helped them over the difficult years. He had read the World Trade Organization's description of Egypt as a 'model country for speedy recovery'.

Jake was thinking that he must take a couple of painkillers to speed his own recovery. Mary was avoiding another visit to the tempting dish of pastries.

The red speed boat was tied to the jetty, already equipped with twin engines running, when the family arrived just before ten. Mahmoud sat on the boat, holding her steady as they climbed on board.

'I thank you for being on time,' he said 'and this is your son? We are of similar age, but not height.' He hooted with laughter.

'Yes, I'm Jake, specially grown to play tennis and

basketball,' Jake joked, 'but not to fit easily into coaches or planes.' He towered above the lad as the two shook hands. Then Mahmoud jumped ashore asking them to take care and wishing them good luck. He would see them later.

'Would it be OK with you if I take off on one ski from the end of the jetty? It's the right height,' Jake asked his father, and watched as Alex gently manoeuvered the boat into position. As he sat down he curled three loops of rope into his left hand and Alex drove slowly away. Just before the line tightened Jake signalled with the tow bar, and dropped the loops as the boat accelerated out to sea.

Jake's strong legs flexed as he crossed the waves and wake, almost brushing the sea with his shoulder as he leaned over to pull himself far right of the boat; then turning, jumping and shifting all his weight he crossed to the left side. He zigzagged in this way for ten minutes while Alex took them in a gradual semi-circle parallel to the beach.

Suddenly Jake dropped the line and sank slowly into the sea.

'He's off!' shouted Mary, who had been watching the skier's every move. 'He didn't fall. Quickly, go back and see what the problem is.'

'Hey, why did you drop off?' called Alex as they approached their swimming son. 'Are you all right?'

'I'm fine. I just wanted to take a closer look at that old yacht over there. I tried to signal, but mom didn't see me.'

A relieved Alex told him to climb up via the transom, circled round to pick up the floating ski, and drove over to the dirty boat. The boat was jerking and pulling on a short chunky chain like an overgrown puppy, straining to be free.

'She looks very in-ter-es-ting,' Jake drawled, rubbing himself down with a towel. 'Let's go on board.'

Mary looked around. 'Better not. It would be trespassing. They can see us from the shore.'

'Oh Mom, you are not going to spoil *this* adventure are you?' Jake asked.

'If we board on the other side no one will know. Besides there is a 'for sale' sign on the door ... let's go,' Alex shouted as they sped round to the starboard side of the yacht. They noted her name, *Carina*, on the wheelhouse as they tied up fore and aft alongside and clambered on board. Alex gave Mary a helping hoist.

Running her hand along the broken rail Mary commented that this would be an elegant ship once all the salt and sand was washed away. Jake was busy peering through the dusty windows. 'Hardly a ship, more like a luxury yacht, I would say. Hey, look at the mess inside. Must have been broken-into and totalled.'

'That's just what I was thinking. She is very old and narrow in the beam; maybe from the forties, and with a German profile. Just like many of the guests in our hotel,' Alex joked.

'How about taking down the name and number of the agent and asking him what goes?' Jake suggested. 'It's just the kind of boat that we dig, Dad.'

Mary joined them after pacing the decks, and caught the last comment. 'I hope you two aren't getting big ideas. We couldn't possibly own a boat like this. Much too much for us.' Nevertheless, as they climbed back into the red peril she suggested that the two men went to see the agent while she looked up *Carina* on the laptop; showing a modicum of interest at least.

'I hope you won't spoil this, Mary,' Alex quietly warned as they re-entered the harbour. 'Not only is it a vessel with character – more interesting than anything else we have seen here – but her story could lead to a great book.'

'Cool,' quipped Jake.

Having tied up the ski boat and seen Mary off to the hotel, Alex and Jake looked for the yacht brokerage. A passer-by directed them towards the mini-market; they would find the broker next door to the real estate office.

The streets were baking in the midday sun, and it was a relief to enter the broker's air-conditioned building, after a perfunctory glance at the many boats advertised in the window.

The agent, a small man with a huge chair and a boardroom-sized desk, was chatting on an old black phone and swivelling his chair from side to side. He motioned to the two to sit in the chairs opposite and stubbed out his smoking cigarette.

'Yes, I'll see to that for you. I must go now ... I have clients in the office. Yes, leave it to me, sir.' He put his hand over his mouth and droopy moustache and told them in a loud whisper that he would attend to them very soon; yet continued his conversation for another five minutes before his final 'Salut'.

'Your name is Johnson – a very famous name. Where are you from? Where do you stay? How long for? Are you relatives? Which boat would you like to buy? Would you want to try any yachts? Or are you hiring? My name is Ahmed; pleased to do business with you.'

Alex told his life story in a nutshell, quickly before he was interrupted with further questions, and what they were interested in viewing.

'We were water skiing and noticed the old boat out on a mooring. She looked to have been abandoned. What is she doing here?'

Ahmed smiled, still swinging, and prepared to tell his tale; first taking his phone off its cradle.

'It is an amazing history. She is over seventy years old, built for the Nazi Goëring before World War Two...'

Three

Back in his hotel suite Alex researched this story using his laptop, beginning with the building of *Karin II* in 1937, and began to write his own version of the history he discovered.

'On that April day the Hamburg newspapers were filled with details of the forthcoming launch of a yacht which had been built for Field Marshal Hermann Goëring. Ninety feet long, seventy tons in weight and built from oak diagonal timbers overlaid with Rangoon teak planking. She was the grandest leisure vessel ever to be built in their yards; designed to be a symbol of German shipbuilding supremacy, costing an astounding 1.3 million reichmarks.

Crowds were already gathering around the launching ramps and along the Rhine river-banks as Goëring and his new wife Emmy Sonnemann arrived in their cream, straight eight imported Buick, with red leather seats and detail. The gentle applause that greeted them rose to a roar as Emmy, who had been a popular actress, stepped down from the limo wrapping her fur trimmed coat around her. The breeze was still chilly. As they entered the thirty-foot high boat shed they were passed by scurrying workmen in overalls, making last minute adjustments on to the magnificent hull. As the couple walked around the stern they found that *Carina* had been scrolled in large gold lettering on the transom.

'Your first wife died seven years ago and you already have our home named after her; why the yacht too, Hermann?' Emmy asked.

'Not this again!' he answered. 'I have told you before – she was very special, like the yacht, and died so young.'

'Yes, but now I should be your "special". Remember this was a wedding gift for both of us.'

'I have no wish to discuss this any further, with all these people listening,' he told her. Looking around he said, 'Besides, it's time for the launch. Remember to smile; I see the cameramen have arrived.'

Goëring, dressed in his enormous white uniform with rows of medals and gold braiding, paced around like the tame lion he had at home as a pet. He shouted for the yard manager to expedite the launch and to bring them the Champagne for the ceremony. Handing the bottle to Emmy he told her to be careful not to dent the hull, yet to smash her hard enough to break the bottle; it would be bad luck if it didn't break the first time. The bottle was tied to the wide ribbon that hung from the railing above their heads. Emmy took hold of it and nervously swung the bottle at the hull. There was a hush in the shed; she had not smashed the bottle.

'Oh, maybe that is because I forgot to name her...' Emmy cried.

After muttering to himself, 'Incompetent bitch!', he told her that he could make allowances for her mistake as she was only an actress and often didn't listen to his instructions.

'Here, hand me the bottle,' he demanded.

'No, it is my job and that is what my fans would want.' She swung the bottle more vigorously the second time and it shattered against the shiny eight coats of paint. 'I name this yacht *Carina*. May God bless her and all who sail in her!' Emmy said, projecting her voice above the noise of the crowd. The vessel slid down the metal ramps, accelerated and hit the water with an enormous splash, displacing water, which rolled towards the river banks and soaked many of the onlookers.

As a crew of sailors secured the vessel to a jetty, Goëring jumped on board and stood on the aft deck waving to the exultant crowds. Emmy slipped quietly inside the wheelhouse and down the steps into the saloon, where workmen were unpacking the many boxes that they had carried on board. Emmy helped them store the gold tableware, crystal glasses and crested china before four men carried in a large table and four green leather arm chairs to match the leather built-in sofa. Goëring had arrived and walked around the saloon with his hands on his hips sticking out his rotund stomach, smiling and silently watching the whole process.

When the men had finished their task and left, Emmy walked up to him, put her arms round his neck, and asked, 'Do we need all this precious cargo? Imagine what will happen if we venture out in rough weather.'

'We will be entertaining our Leader and all the Generals at this important time in our history. We must have the very best of everything. We have earned it: you with your twenty years on the stage and me with my years of service to the Fatherland.'

'I hardly ever see you. If it isn't hunting, or partying or warmongering in those private meetings with Hitler and his henchmen you are working for all your businesses. Will we ever have more time to ourselves?' Emmy asked him.

Roughly removing her arms he replied, 'I have had enough of your complaining today. You must be tired. Go to the master cabin and try out our new bathroom facilities; rest and I will join you later.'

Emmy winced as her husband forced his huge bulk up against her, pushing her against the centre table.

They hastily parted as a team of electricians arrived to fit a bank of radio-telephone equipment above the chart table in the wheelhouse. Emmy disappeared to her cabin as ordered.

Carefully, Goëring removed a brown paper parcel from his briefcase and, taking care that no one was looking, lifted a centre panel from the table top and placed the package in the recess. He quickly realigned the table on hearing the sound of heavy footsteps on the deck above. He snapped to attention, giving the Nazi salute, as two of his fellow officers stepped down into the saloon and returned his welcome with 'Heil Hitler'.

The two officers were Field Marshal Kesselring, a close friend of Goëring and Commander of the German Army, and Admiral Dönitz who was Commander of Submarines. Both refused the offered whisky, saying that it could wait until after their discussions, and pulled their chairs up to the table.

'We have important developments to share with you,' Dönitz told Goëring, who walked to the side table and took several pills with a slug of liquor. The other two looked at each other and raised their eyebrows as he sat and spread his bulky frame on the built-in leather couch.

'What a fine ship,' Kesselring said, looking admiringly around at the bourgeois elegance. 'Congratulations. Will you be using her as your business centre?'

'That is my idea. She is safe, protected by guards, and it is sheltered from storms in the docks. She is mobile and more spacious than my train. I have even had a double-size toilet fitted. She will be delivered to Berlin whenever I am there. As you can see I have equipped her with all the up-to-date communications systems so will be in constant touch with the war progress.'

Kesselring swept his baton over a map he had placed on the table and tapped various countries as he talked. 'We are making good progress. At this very moment my troops are marching into Austria. The Austrians are celebrating ... as they desired they are now a province of Germany. Just as Hitler predicted, the Anschluss has begun.'

'And Russia?' Goëring asked.

'All is not what it seems with the Russians. They are talking of a pact with Britain and France, but I believe they may secretly sign up with us. My plans allow for a large troop build-up on the borders. We must be well prepared.'

Admiral Dönitz looked at each man in turn. 'You must consider my problems also. The Fuhrer promised he would establish Naval bases for my submarines. We are developing the new Type VII U-boats. We will need dockage soon...'

'Ah. He plans to strike Denmark and Norway. There he can establish a strong Navy, using their extensive fleet alongside ours, with which to attack England,' said Kesselring.

At this point Goëring, who had been leaning back in his chair with a half smile on his face as if in another world, became agitated. 'But we need to annex Belgium, Holland and Luxembourg ... more ports and more moorings.'

'My men will be spread thin. We will need plenty of air support from you, Hermann,' Kesselring told him.

Goëring leant forward. 'You will have seen from my publicity film ... the skies will be filled with our efficient Air Force. As Supreme Commander of the Luftwaffe I can assure you both that we will win the coming war. When we Germans control Europe we will then, as Hitler tells me, conquer America.'

'We have planned it all,' he shouted, 'now that the Army has joined the service of the Party all will work for the overthrow of the world. Whatever it takes.'

'We both agree,' Dönitz told him. 'There is only one slight problem – the codes.'

'What codes are you talking about?' Goëring asked.

'The Enigma Code machines are being produced in Poland and I am very concerned that some may find their way into the hands of our enemies. There are a number of Polish traitors escaping to Britain.'

Goëring did not believe this. 'They will never crack our codes; they are too complex. Your submarines will be able to destroy the American convoys without the British being able to locate them.'

'I don't know about that,' Dönitz said. 'Our man in their Ministry of Defence believes they are working on something very secret...'

Clearly distressed, Goëring walked over to the side table once more and washed down another handful of pills with a large glass of whisky. The decanter slipped through his hand and smashed on the floor. The noise was such that Emmy appeared at the top of the steps in a lacy nightgown.

'What was that?' she asked, looking pale and shocked. 'Oh Hermann, what happened? Let me clean up the mess for you.'

A red-faced Goering turned on her. 'I told you to stay in the cabin until I joined you, didn't I? How dare you appear in front of my guests dressed like that? Have you been listening to our conversation? Go back to your room at once.'

'Oh, I am so sorry gentlemen ... I had no idea you were here ... it was the noise...' Emmy stammered, and humiliated she backed away.

Despite her inexperience of the high life, Emmy proved to be a good second wife and her husband soon learnt to keep her from his responsibilities, evil undertakings and problems. It seems from her later writings that she did not see his ruthless and brutal side in their private world as often as his genial nature. After the birth of a late child, a daughter who was named Edda (not after

Mussolini's daughter as widely thought, but a friend of Emmy's) she spent most of her time at her home, Carinhall, north east of Berlin. Naturally, she never publically acknowledged his responsibility for the corrupt, criminal and macabre nature of the Nazi regime but refused to become a member of the Party. It was easier to blame Hitler, knowing how completely devoted to him her husband had always been. Yet she must have been fully aware of the Nazi solution to 'The Jewish Problem' as she helped many of her theatre friends to escape from Germany, and was generous with funds and creature comforts for the needy. These were acts that she knew could put her own family in danger.

The previous year Goëring had been appointed by Hitler as Plenipotentiary for the implementation of his Four Year Plan. Now he set about creating the Hermann Goëring Works, which was a giant industrial nexus of 700,000 workers and allowed him to accumulate an enormous fortune. He flaunted his wealth in his taste for extravagant apparel and precious jewellery, his home, hunting lodge, cars, railway and yacht. Meanwhile, many of his people were expected to give up everything for the war effort.

Carina became a floating Embassy for the State where world leaders, royalty and diplomats were entertained. There were secret meetings with Hitler, Himmler, Heydrich and Bormann. Other prominent Nazis were invited for coffee and cakes. Emmy was a popular hostess with the help of their butler Robert and a crew in Air Force uniforms. Diamond daggers, the legendary Mauser pistol and valuable paintings adorned the cabins, two saloons and library. The couple hosted lavish dinner parties with fine wines and vintage cognac; often after duck and seagull shoots, which were taboo for seamen in those times. Their Sèvres porcelain with their gold family crest, the silver service and drinking cups, and monogrammed ashtrays were in constant use. There were official reviews of the German Fleet and movement up and down the inland waterways for official business and pleasure cruising, but it was not until the start of the war in 1939 that *Carina* became Goëring's personal control centre. With his boat anchored near the Luftwaffe headquarters in Berlin he was able to sit in privacy on his leather sofa in the panelled saloon and study operational details on the burr walnut table.

By July 1944 Goëring had been sidelined by Hitler and his disciples. On his yacht he sank into lethargy and a world of illusions. He was described as a bloated shadow of himself; discredited, isolated and taking the brunt of the blame for Germany's defeat.

Though he had said many times that he wanted to dictate the new order in Europe by 'diplomatic' means he had played a key role in the Anschluss in 1938 and bludgeoning the Czechs into submission. When he was put in charge of National Defence in 1939, and designated Hitler's successor, he had directed the Luftwaffe campaigns against Poland and France, and was promoted to Field Marshal. The following year he directed a full offensive against Britain, called 'Operation Eagle', in order to drive the RAF from the skies and secure the British surrender. But his Luftwaffe failed, and the planned invasion of England was cancelled. Hitler never forgave him.

He was sitting on his specially built seat on the deck of *Carina* as a German staff car drove up to the dock and Dönitz and Kesselring were helped out by their driver. They had come to see him for the last time. As Dönitz stepped onto the gangplank to board the boat, and walked towards him, Goering swung around, pointing his rifle at him, and asked what they wanted.

'I know you would like to use that Hermann,' said Dönitz. 'You have never liked me have you? Put it away. Things are bad enough for us without another death. Both my sons, Peter and Klaus, have been killed in this terrible war. I have little left to live for.'

Goëring lowered the gun, muttering to himself, and led the two men below into the saloon.

'What news do you have for me?' he asked. 'Are we winning … ha … ha?'

They sat around the leather settee with the table in front of them.

'At sea we are suffering intolerable losses … the enemy seems to hold every trump card. They know all our secrets and we know none of theirs. They must have broken our codes, as I feared they would,' Dönitz told him.

'Yes, they seem to be able to cover all our strategic areas with long-range air patrols, giving no warning. It is all Hitler's fault … for years he refused to let me build my little "Swallow".'

He took a model of the jet from the sideboard and stared at it lovingly before handing it around. 'Now he wants squadrons built in days. It is too late.'

'This Messerschmitt is a wonder,' agreed Dönitz. 'I believe the few we have are claiming hundreds of Allied kills. Those turbo jets can outmanoeuvre anything … and the speed! As you say – too little too late.'

It was Kesselring's turn. 'And what about my soldiers on the Eastern Front? You did not send the air cover that was promised. As you say the losses … the Yaks and Migs are running free. The way things are going the Commies will end up controlling half of Europe. And have you heard the rumours of a coup being planned against the Fuhrer?'

'No. You had better not tell me who is involved. However, if it succeeds I am ready to lead Germany to victory.'

Dönitz disagreed. 'I know you have been named as

Deputy in the past, but Hitler is angry about the mistakes of your bombers ... how could you have dropped on London by mistake? I thought we were aiming to demolish all their control centres. Besides, if the Leadership is changed I have more experience ... indeed I am your senior.'

Goëring sat, stony-faced, as he bore their accusations. Recently he had been avoiding Hitler's briefings; they were too painful. His radio and telegraph communications on the boat had been feeding him with all the distressing news he could stomach. He knew that the terrible cold winters on the Russian borders had prevented his planes from dropping vital supplies. He had been attempting to keep Hitler happy for years with misinformation about his Luftwaffe capabilities. He had too few planes covering too many theatres of war, and his technical staff had let him down.

For the next hour Hermann attempted to justify his position to his two visitors (he could no longer count anyone as a friend), and was bringing them much needed brandy when sirens wailed followed by loud explosions. The smell of cordite and smoke quickly reached them as they sat in silence, holding their breath. The roar of a low flying bomber formation grew ever nearer. It was overhead.

The yacht was fully camouflaged, and they did not receive a direct hit, but Kesselring and Dönitz panicked and rose to leave.

'We are not safe here,' Kesselring warned. 'Let's get the hell out of it. Quick, we will make for the nearest bunker. This boat will be a target.'

They both ran for their car and drove away. Goëring was left sitting at the table, alone, his head in his hands. He was stroking the table, wondering, when there was a huge explosion.

* * *

The leaders of the Hitler's Reich were 'asleep on watch' when, a year later, failures of the German intelligence network led to their annihilation. The largest Armada ever of ships, boats, and floating concrete Mulberry harbours crossed the Channel from the south of England heading for the beaches of Normandy on 6th June 1945, while Goëring and Hitler celebrated Edda Goëring's sixth birthday at Carinhall.

Admiral Dönitz's Navy failed to attack the invasion force off the Isle of Wight or the Channel entrance, as planned. The last U-boats of Hitler's 'Operation Neptune' were unable to sink any of the invasion fleet. Kesselring's German troops were in retreat in Italy and powerless to combat the last Red Army offensive on the Eastern front. Goëring's Luftwaffe only possessed 300 planes as against 11,000 Allied aircraft; as a result of long wrangling over aircraft design, production and use.

German resistance on D-Day inflicted 'only fleabites', as Dönitz later admitted.

Four

'So those were some of the Goëring's experiences on his yacht,' Jake commented. 'She was just a war machine.'

The family walked towards the Seventh Star Café on the promenade of the El Gouna Marina which, they had been told, was a popular meeting place for the great and the good. It was certainly crowded and buzzing with the chatter of the international Jet Set, Alex replied after they had settled at the last outside table overlooking the bay.

'I had to imagine the scenes. Ahmed the Broker lent me Emmy's memoirs - *Life with Goëring* - and there was no mention of *Carina*. Reading between the lines I tried to envisage what her life was really like. Imagine a middle-aged actress giving up her career to marry one of the most powerful men in Germany, only to find that she had to draw a veil over the life he was leading. She was unable to say how much she resented the power Hitler had over him or admit to any knowledge of the many atrocities that they, and the party, perpetrated.

'Admittedly in those days women were completely under their husband's thumb, but her book seems to be a complete whitewash; maybe even a public relations exercise to present the Goëring family in a favourable light. She said that it took her a long time to discover what her husband really thought as he preferred to talk of theatre, books, paintings and human relationships. She believed that a woman in love thinks only of her partner's success, and it is of little importance to her how he obtains it. But how could this be true?'

'Many of our own American stars have had similar tragic experiences, according to the films based on their lives. Men the world over have behaved like beasts; think of Doris Day or Marilyn Monroe,' said Mary.

'I agree, but the circumstances were different. When Emmy met Goëring he owned mansions, estates and castles in Austria, Germany and Poland. He had been an air-ace in World War 1, and was now at the height of his power as Commander-in-Chief of the German Air Force. He was responsible for organising the rapid build-up of the aircraft industry and training their pilots. He had, however, many weird quirks. He pursued extravagant tastes in clothing; changing uniforms or suits four or five times a day on which he wore rows of medals and extravagant jewellery.

'He organised State hunts with feasts to follow at which he dressed in vast leather breeches and a ridiculously small hat with a feather. Whereas he thought of himself as a Renaissance man, he became enormously overweight, the butt of many jokes, and became totally corrupted by power and ambition. Doctors have written that behind the genial façade was a brutal, cunning and flawed man.'

'He seems to have had a very complex personality and you seem to be totally immersed in his history.'

'I am, Mary, but it is only one small part of the overall history of *Carina* – one which I am determined to write about.'

'And you seem to be well underway with the research. When we have finished our drinks I would like to walk along the shopping mall, if you don't mind,' said Mary, deliberately changing the subject. 'I have seen some pretty pashas and veils I would like to buy for presents. Maybe we could have supper downtown. It will be cheaper; we can use our Exchange cards.'

'Good idea. We'll come with you. Let me just get the

bill,' said Alex, realising that war and evil men were not amongst Mary's favourite topics.

'I'm famished,' Jake told them as they walked past the museum, 'and I have another question. How did the yacht survive the bombing, do you know, Dad?'

'Here, let's sit at that bar terrace next to the Mall to wait for Mom, and I'll tell you. Is that OK, Mary?'

'Yes fine, I won't be long,' Mary replied before heading for the shops.

Once she had rounded the corner, Alex ordered two beers.

'The answer to your question is that Goëring managed to hide the boat at the end of the war. He was near to his home when captured by the Americans in 1945, and jailed. I read the details of the Nuremburg Trials and their aftermath. When he heard the Court's Judgment he swallowed a cyanide pill he had hidden in his wash bag, to avoid the humiliation of being hanged. After what he called his 'eight glorious years' on *Carina*, he left her not knowing whether he would ever board her again.'

Mary returned with several packages just as the waiter arrived with drinks and a platter of local delicacies. Alex ordered a glass of wine for his wife before adding 'Now you are back I can tell you both the fun part of the story. Would you believe who the next owners were?'

Jake and Mary shook their heads. 'Guess'.

'Well, err … the Russians?'

'It couldn't have been, stupid, they were hundreds of miles away,' said Mary.

'Could it have been the Brits then?'

'Yes, but better still, it was the British Royal Navy and their King George.'

Jake choked and spat out his mouthful into a nearby plant pot 'What the hell was that? Sorry.' he gasped.

'Sheep's eyes I think. Didn't you like them?' Alex asked, laughing.

'I thought you choked at the thought of "our yacht" once belonging to Royalty,' Mary commented as Jake gulped down a glass of iced water.

'Did I hear Mom say "our yacht"? Has she changed her mind? Does she think *Carina* could be ours?' Alex asked Jake, winking.

'No, not at all. There is no way we could manage the finances. We have to save for your college fees Jake, remember. Let's face facts. We are just following a great story for Dad's next book. How was the yacht transferred from the Nazi to the King? It seems a little far-fetched.'

'It seems that, at the end of the war, Montgomery's men discovered her, undamaged, in an estuary of the Rhine.'

'Now, let me think ... Montgomery was that bossy Brit guy who always crossed Patton, wasn't he? Some General?'

'You are right, Jake. After successes in Africa, Field Marshal Montgomery was given command of the Twenty-First Army for the invasion of mainland Europe, and fought with the Allies in Normandy and the Battle of the Bulge in Belgium. They advanced to the north defeating the Germans and forcing the surrender at Lüneburg Heath after crossing the Rhine in March 1945. Shortly after that, they discovered *Carina*.'

'Have you written about Montgomery yet?' Mary asked him. 'If so I would like to proofread for you. Maybe we can walk back to the hotel now and have a rest before visiting one or two night spots.'

'I was hoping for an early night,' Jake told them. 'Remember I head off on my adventure to Luxor at five o'clock tomorrow morning. In the evening I hope to sail down the river in a felucca and the day after I will be visiting the Komombo temple, which is full of crypts, passages and shrines to their gods and kings. Doesn't it sound great! Our tour group will be away for three days so you can explore the night life while I am gone.'

They walked back over a Venetian style hump-backed bridge and through the beautifully manicured gardens. Each was thinking that this was not at all the holiday they had envisioned. It was so weird to have the past spreading like a cumulus cloud over their lives. They had little to talk to each other about – except Jake. Neither was inclined to share their innermost thoughts with the other. They had no real desire to touch each other either.

Back on the balcony Mary sat down to read the next chapter of her husband's work, pencil in hand ready to correct any typos. As she leafed through the file she found a scene with the Royal Family had been added. Great – he seems really switched on to this project, she thought, popping another sugared almond into her mouth. It did not occur to her that the pages she was reading would have a great influence on her husband's emotional life. She had never bothered to listen to him when he had tried to share that terrible burden of mourning his family. Hey, what was done was done she thought; there's no point in moping.

Five

The British Twenty-First Army, alongside the Canadian and American forces, had just taken part in 'Operation Overlord' – the invasion of German-controlled Normandy. They had then advanced to the Rhine where they were resting and recuperating after the German surrender. World War II was effectively over but there was much work ahead of them. There were few trees left for shelter and the air was still cold on this day in May 1945. The soldiers had only recently erected the large mess tents, encircled by groups of smaller tents in the style of a village, with main throughways. Heavy rain was turning the site to a field of mud and soldiers scurried from one area to another, attempting to hop over puddles and rivulets.

Montgomery's mobile office, with sleeping quarters and radio equipment, had followed the fighting front for the sweep through Germany and had now come to rest on raised ground near to the main entrance road. Monty, as he was affectionately called by his men, was a short dapper man with a well-trimmed moustache and loud high-pitched voice which resonated with self-confidence. This, together with his single mindedness, had an infectious quality, which affected all ranks in the Armed Forces and the general public: a vital asset when the Alliance had been forged.

Hitler had ordered a massive attack, using three armies to attempt to destabilize the Accord and take Antwerp where their supplies were landing. The Germans were more powerful for the first two days but soon ran out of fuel for their tanks and equipment and the clearing skies enabled the superior Allied air power to prevail. Wherever Monty walked on the site, dressed in Army battledress and his black beret with two badges (one for the Royal Tank Regiment and the other the British Officer's badge) his troops would snap to attention and salute. He always carried his Field Marshal's baton, which he slapped against his leg to emphasize a point when addressing his men. He was talking to his adjutant, slapping away, when a uniformed dispatch rider, on his Royal Enfield motorbike, swerved through the mud and came to a sliding stop. He dismounted, leant his mud-caked bike against the office wall, saluted the two officers and handed the adjutant a bundle of mail.

'Sir, I have a message from your troupe up the road – about a mile away. They have found something ... they would like you to investigate.'

'What is it?' Monty asked him, 'ammunition, or a crashed Messerschmitt?'

'No sir, I believe it is some sort of boat or barge, on the river.'

Montgomery turned to his adjutant and, pointing with his baton, told him to organize four men and a jeep to lead them to the site; then check the area for mines before investigating the find.

The boggy ground leading to the river bank prevented the jeep and Montgomery's staff car – an open chauffeur-driven Humber limo with a four star plate to the front and flying a Union Jack pennant – from parking too near to the long dirty-green shape moored there. After a bomb-disposal man had checked the area the two officers walked up to the hulk, half-submerged in the reeds. They watched as the soldiers pulled away and folded a number of tarpaulins, and replaced the boarding ladder, which had been lying alongside the vessel.

The adjutant walked the plank and stood on the deck with Montgomery following close behind. He stamped his feet and tapped the super-structure before trying to open the wheelhouse door. Then, turning to his aide he ordered, 'Tell my chauffeur to fetch the bolt croppers from the boot of my car. We must see inside,' quietly adding 'This is important; I do believe she could have been Goëring's private yacht. We will see. Here, have a go.'

The enthusiastic chauffeur cut away the chain for them and the officers entered. They studied the up-to-date fittings in the wheelhouse and the banks of communication equipment around the navigation table and in the saloon, peering at the craft and valuable artifacts displayed on the counter tops. Monty opened cupboards and drawers, closely investigating their precious contents before declaring:

'There is no doubt at all who this boat belonged to. It looks as if Goëring had to make a quick getaway. He has left everything in place.'

'Unbelievable!' agreed his aide. 'Look at this operational map with all the arrows marking their plans for the war. It is hard to believe, but from here he must have directed the Luftwaffe campaigns against Poland and France and the great offensive against Britain.'

'And ordered those bombing errors which gave us time to recover control of our stations. From this very room those instructions lost him the war,' Monty added before leaving the room, pacing the aft deck and, having located the key, visiting the owner's cabin.

When he returned he declared, 'I have decided to requisition this yacht for the use of the Royal Navy Rhine Flotilla. She will make a good review ship and also serve as a suitable boat for the King. Inform Headquarters when we return to camp and organize a Navy crew to look after her forthwith. They can move her up to our yard on the river.'

'Sir! She is certainly beautifully equipped, fit for a King and his family,' agreed his adjutant and pointed out a wall plaque. 'Look she was a gift in 1937 from a grateful German Nation to Goëring and his wife Emmy – I wonder how those people feel about them now. Certainly not "grateful".'

'I believe he was popular with the people,' Monty replied. 'He appeared to be so different from Hitler; far more genial. In fact that big, noisy person was totally corrupt, and signed all the documents on these shelves that sealed the fate of millions. He made promises to protect them, and let them down. He tried to justify killing Jews and the disabled. He was directly responsible for the SS and the Austrian Anschluss which started the war.'

The adjutant nodded. 'Yes, and at the same time it was said that he was more interested in fancy costumes, yachting and hunting than his Air Force and aerial combat. He seems to have had a split personality. The Yanks are trying to cure his heroin addiction in jail. I can't think why. He must be for the chop, and soon.'

Montgomery opened a low cupboard under the side-deck, brought out a bottle of Cognac and read the label. Then he took down two glasses from a teak glass holder, saying with a certain amount of pleasure, 'The best! There are boxes of fine wine here also. A toast – to the end of Nazi Germany and peace in Europe, together with the King.' Together they raised their glasses and repeated 'The King'.

A huge white ensign was flying high from the flagstaff, mounted on the yacht's transom, as she cruised up the Rhine towards the distant hillside town of Heidelberg, in Germany, 1959. The name *Carina* had long since been erased and *The Royal Albert* had recently been replaced in large gold letters with *Prince Charles* in honour of the British Queen's first son. The Prince's courtesy flag was waving from the cross-trees of the mast and she was dressed overall with semaphore flags, a sign of celebration.

It had been a delightful summer's day and a light evening breeze cooled the guests as they sipped German hock and chatted nineteen to the dozen; sharing experiences of the season's sporting events and spreading social gossip. A trio played popular current tunes on the aft deck as Prince Philip in his Naval uniform, and his young son, moved from group to group laughing at their stories and jokes.

Under a vast canopy on the aft deck the ship's captain was talking to Princess Margaret and her companion David Pope, an antiques dealer. All three held Champagne flutes.

'My posting is almost at an end,' the Captain was telling the Princess. 'I shall miss the yacht and the many trips we have taken ... north to Holland and south to Switzerland on several occasions.'

The only time I have been aboard over the past twelve years and not enjoyed myself,' said the Princess, 'was when we reviewed the Fleet. I was so sick. Remember? She is too narrow for the open seas, but perfect for river cruising.'

'I remember it well. We had to stow everything and still had some breakages. The wheelhouse filled with water when we were caught in heavy seas.' The Captain then added wistfully, 'You will not be having such problems with the new Royal Yacht, Ma'am.'

David wondered whether the *Prince Charles* would become redundant now that *Britannia* had been commissioned.

'Yes I believe so. Just as well. The Queen believes (and this is a delicate subject in these times of hardship) that it is high time for the boat to be returned to the Goëring family,' Margaret replied. 'Besides, it would be much more convenient to have the Royal Yacht moored in Britain.'

Smiling, David joked with her, 'Yes, I remember you had to fly to Frankfurt and be collected in the Rolls Royce to drive to Wiesbaden. Very time consuming. Now you will just be whistled on board at the most convenient port.'

After giving him a decidedly dirty look Margaret said, 'Ah, excuse me, I must go and talk to Lady Chatsworth,' and gently nudged through the crowd as the two men watched her walk away.

'The Queen must worry that her people would disapprove if they knew her family owned and used a Nazi vessel all through these years of post-war austerity,' David suggested.

'I hear that the Goëring family has decided that they do not want her either. They will accept her on delivery and then sell her.'

'Really, well I may know someone who would be interested in buying the yacht. She is just what he has been looking for. Will you send me the details when you have them?' David asked.

'Certainly, sir. The buffet has been served in the saloon. You had better join the others.'

David walked up to Prince Charles and tapped his arm. Charles smiled as he saw who it was, shook hands and watched as the waiter filled up David's glass. At ten years old, dressed in a blazer and grey slacks, Charles could pass for a teenager; especially when conversing with adults.

'Not you again, you old bounder,' said the young prince. 'Good to see you. Will you be racing at Cowes next month? If so, I would love to sail with you for a race or two.'

'Yes, but not sailing,' replied David. 'I have agreed to co-pilot in a friend's power boat for the Cowes-Torquay race. By the way, congratulations on having the yacht named after you. Last year you were still in short shorts and peeling potatoes to help the cook! What a difference a year makes.'

'Come on you two, supper is served!' Margaret called, and they joined her. Margaret took David's arm and flirted with him as she led the way into the saloon.

A crowd of people surrounded the centre table, laden with a delicious selection of fish, meats, fruits and pastries. They were helping themselves to food and wine from the counter top and moved aside for the Royals to join them.

David whispered to Margaret as they approached, 'Do you fancy some peace on our own later, when they have all gone?'

'I can't wait. As you know I have had a difficult time lately. I found the … my decision not to marry Peter … so hard. We had planned it for a long time. I am only just beginning to live again.'

'I can help you "live a little" as the song goes,' he suggested.

'Certainly,' the Princess answered, 'but I have a secret to impart. I have been spending time with a new man. Tony is a society photographer and I have asked him to stay on board for our cruise on the River Elbe to Dresden. He will be able to make a photographic record of the whole trip. He has a cheeky sense of humour and a leisurely lifestyle which is such a contrast to my formal duties.'

'If you mean Armstrong-Jones, I have met him,' David told her. 'He was at Eton with my brother, and my company has printed his work in *Vanity Fair* and American magazines such as *House and Garden* and *Life*. I believe his uncle was Oliver Messel the stage designer.'

'Yes. We first met when he was taking photos of the Queen and Philip before their tour of Canada in 1957,' Margaret told him. 'He has less-than-Royal origins and often uses non-u words, but he is very intense when working and does have connections with Germany. His great grandfather was a well-known Berlin architect; a discipline he studied at Cambridge. Apart from his serious side he is very sexy and I do believe that we are falling in love.'

'Do you think your sister will agree this time? At least he is not a divorcee. I will just top up our glasses so that we can drink to your future.'

Well, well, Mary thought sarcastically – quite a story; and she carefully replaced all the pages in Alex's briefcase. Where will Alex venture next? Maybe he is considering a meticulously planned cruise to Dresden.

She was right. Alex had investigated the archives for any details of the Royal cruises up and down the rivers and canals of Germany, but had discovered nothing. All such details had been expunged, or suppressed in the interests of privacy. He had no access to diaries. So, he read about the river as it was after the war and compared those reports with descriptions of the Saxony of today.

Today, many cruise ships meander along the 400 miles of the River Elbe from Hamburg to Dresden. Their international passengers enjoy the gentle pastoral landscape of Lower Saxony with the Juniper bushes, purple heather and grazing flocks of Heidschucken sheep. They watch the river banks slip past at such a gentle pace that the passengers have time to joke with walkers or cyclists on the river bank and the canoeists they overtake. They begin to befriend fellow tourists and become involved with their surroundings; lifting their binoculars to follow otters, marsh harriers or red kites. They travel through the flat farmlands to reach rolling hilly terrain and then enjoy the delights of the distant mountains and gorges of Saxony-Anhalt. These must be similar experiences to those of the travellers on *Carina* at the end of the fifties. The difference comes, however, when the boats tie up against the town or city walls and the trippers troop ashore to see the sights.

The first city on the *Carina* tour was Magdeburg, which had suffered near total destruction from Allied firebombing only fourteen years earlier and the centre and the old impressive Grunderzeit suburbs had been devastated. The American and Soviet troops occupied the area together for a while but the Americans soon left and the Soviets demolished the few old buildings still standing to re-build in Stalinist neo-classical style. The bodies of the deceased Nazi leaders were buried here before being later incinerated. In the fifties this was a dreary place with gaping spaces, like mouths of rotten teeth, yet to be rebuilt by the German Democratic Republic.

After the reunification of Germany, Magdeburg became the capital of the new State of Saxony-Anhalt, and any visitor's lasting impression is of the ships and barges crossing the world's largest canal bridge. A feat of engineering it is 918 metres long at a cost of 500 million euros and completed in December 2003. It forms the gateway between East and West Germany.

The old Saxon port of Torgau would be the next stop. It was here that the American Sixty-Ninth Infantry Division first met the Soviet soldiers, shook hands and celebrated their joint defeat of Hitler with beer and vodka at the end of World War II, on 25th April 1945. This meeting marked the collapse of Old Germany. Prominent in the Reformation and for the victory of Frederick the Great over the Austrians in 1760 this ancient town did not take kindly to Russian invaders. Today's tourists can be shown round the first Renaissance building in Germany, Hartenfels Castle, which is now open to the public as a museum and enjoy the newfound spirit of unified Germany.

From here the cruise ship visitors can take a coach tour

to nearby Leipzig; the ancient city where Bach was organist and choir director at the Thomaskirke (1685–1750) and Wagner was born (1813). Little has changed over the centuries and musical traditions have been maintained with concerts, opera and theatre attracting many visitors. Allied bombing destroyed the city centre and reconstruction efforts have been slow. In the fifties visitors, driving their own vehicle, would see few buildings still standing; now it is a vibrant place to go.

Dresden, the final destination, is the capital of the State of Saxony dating back to the Neolithic period. Today the pale yellow and green riverside facades of the old style buildings resemble the cityscapes painted by Canaletto in the mid-1700s. Yet there is a photograph of the colossal sculpture by August Schreitmuller overlooking the devastated city in 1945. The figure, dressed in a Roman style gown, is ironically named 'Goodness'. She holds out her hands, palm upwards, towards the completely gutted firebombed buildings. Now this city has been almost completely rebuilt and people can walk through the old town ignorant of the fact that this elegant area has been totally restored. The Opera House, of neo-renaissance architecture, was burnt down in 1945 and an exact replica now stands in its place; rebuilt in 1985. The Zwinger Palace was also rebuilt before reunification and is now a museum housing the Sistine Madonna by Raphael.

Following the fall of the Berlin Wall in 1990 Dresdeners formed an international appeal to help in the rebuilding of the Lutheran Frauenkirche (the baroque Church of our Lady completed in 1743),which had been left in ruins by the Communists. This work took seven years. Using 3D computer technology, architects were able to use old photographs to analyze all the pieces of rubble that had been kept and use them in the reconstruction. The British Queen hosted a concert in Berlin to raise money for the cause and the Duke of Kent, her cousin, attended the consecration. There has been much postwar debate about the tragic destruction of Dresden, a cultural icon, so late in the war. Inquiries concluded that 'the raid had legitimate military ends, brought about by exigent military circumstances'. Many historians disagree.

Alex relived his worst nightmares as he read about the horrors of the war and the long-term consequences; a subject he had not studied in detail before. He found himself shaking as he read the survivors' accounts of the terrible firestorm that followed the dropping of high-explosive bombs known as 'blockbusters', and the incendiaries that followed, on the medieval city of Dresden. Their shocking descriptions used the words 'explosion after explosion', 'inconceivable panic', 'falling ruins', 'cremated adults shrunk to the size of children', 'whole families burnt to death', 'the hot wind of the firestorm threw people back into the burning houses they were trying to escape from', 'lacking oxygen people fainted and were burnt to cinders', 'insane fear gripped me', 'an estimated death toll was between 24,000 and 40,000'. These same words had been used in newspaper accounts of the 'Fire of Lavender Cottage' and how five members of his own family had been wiped from the face of the Earth.

Would he ever get over this tragedy? Only if he could talk out his horrific nightmares.

Six

It was the last day of their holiday and Alex's thoughts of war had made him restless. The previous evening he had been able to put it to one side, as he listened to his son's vivid stories of the trip across the baking desert to the old world of the Nile. He had been amused by Jake's ability to contrast the ancient Thebes, which had been the great cemetery of the Valley of the Kings, with the modern day town of Luxor.

He compared the hundreds of scantily dressed tourists from the cruise ships with the young Muslim women in their full-length black gauze dresses and colourful flowing veils. He had noticed that the hastily organized temple tours were guided by ill-informed youths with poor English; so different from the tours taken in the nineteenth century by culture loving, multilingual, well read, formally dressed Victorian visitors. The town was untidy, dirty and infested with flies, unlike El Gouna; leathery-faced men sat around staring at the visitors or badgered them to buy their wares. Older women crisscrossed the streets carrying bundles or jugs on their heads. The children were virtually naked and had bare feet.

Alex was glad to have given the trip a miss and was delighted that Jake had enjoyed the experience; even sitting and chatting to a pretty Dutch teenager on the coach trip back. Jake was a boy no longer; how quickly he had become a man. Maybe he should be encouraged to study anthropology rather than archaeology?

Now leaving Jake and Mary to sleep, Alex took a leisurely

swim in the hotel pool, partly packed his suitcase and finished reading his notes. Then he decided to walk to the Yacht Agency in town and talk to Ahmed once again. He was welcomed with an unexpected hug and a small dark cup of coffee and they sat on low couches at the end of the office.

'Sugar?' queried Ahmed. 'We drink our coffee very strong and sweet, as you will have found. Sorry but I had no tea. Most visitors here drink tea.'

'This is fine, thank you Ahmed,' Alex told him. 'When in Rome...'

'What do you mean?'

'It is just a saying we have. It means that tourists should try to behave like the locals, not the other way round.'

'I see. Tell me Mr Johnson, do you want to purchase *Carina*? I have another interested party: a sheikh who will be visiting soon. We should tie up this sale, you and me.'

Alex sipped his coffee and looked around at the photos of yachts displayed on the walls and dividing boards and decided to play this along. There were so many craft of all shapes and sizes for sale; surely there could not be much competition for Carina.

'My wife and I cannot make a decision without talking to our bank,' he told the agent. 'As we fly home tomorrow I should be able to fax you with our answer by next week.' He then added, rather sarcastically, 'Let's hope this is soon enough. After all, she has been floating here for many years without finding someone to care for her.'

'I see no problem. Give me your address and contact numbers and I'll let you know if there is another buyer. Would you like me to take you and your family to the airport tomorrow?'

'That would be great,' said Alex removing a card from his wallet and handing it over. 'I will be able to return the hire car at the hotel tonight. We have hardly used it. Nobody told us that the town was a car-free zone.'

'What time is your flight?' the agent asked, as he rose and collected the cups.

'We'll need to be there around ten o'clock; is that OK?'

'I will be at your hotel at nine tomorrow morning and I hope we can do business soon.'

Alex entered the cool cathedral-high hotel atrium to find every desk packed with recent arrivals. He motioned that he was in a hurry to the hire car representative, pointing to his watch, who attended to him before the crowd.

'When will you be returning your car, Mister? I have many customers, as you can see.'

'Oh, I thought you were giving me special treatment!' he told the man.

'You will be pleased to hear that you can have the car now, as I have a lift to the airport tomorrow.' Delving into the pocket of his jeans he produced the keys and handed them over with a quick 'thanks'.

Mary was placing stacks of neatly folded clothes into her suitcase and Jake was on the balcony with his laptop when Alex returned to the apartment.

'Hi, I'm back,' he called and then sank onto the uncluttered half of the four-poster bed. 'All went well. I managed to stall him, but he says that there is someone else in the running…'

'Well we know that's not true. Just the old ruse to keep a buyer hot.' Mary said.

'He offered to take us to the airport tomorrow and I couldn't refuse, so I have returned the car.'

'Here a minute, Dad,' Jake called from the balcony, 'while you were out I found something great.'

'What's that?'

'Look, I have found an article about the yacht. It is written by a German journalist, giving the names of all the owners. Seems the last three are still living. You could interview them about their experiences.'

'Great,' said Alex as he settled down to read the on-screen details and Jake left him in peace.

The following morning the hotel manager was rubbing his hands together as he approached the Johnson family, waiting in the hotel entrance lobby surrounded by their luggage. After greeting them and asking if they had enjoyed their time in his magnificent hotel, and the beautiful resort of El Gouna, he began to ask about their interest in the German boat.

Alex cut him off with 'Ah, here is our lift, we mustn't keep him waiting.' Taking the manager to one side he shook hands, exchanged a large note, and added, 'I'll be back, thanks.' They left via the revolving door, with a small boy trailing behind wheeling their heavy luggage cart.

After a week back at home the Johnson family had fully recovered from the journey, the heat and the excitement of Egypt. They returned to find that summer had arrived early in St Augustine. Living on the north-east coast of Florida they were used to four seasons, although spring and fall lasted only a few weeks and summer sun shone from May to November; with regular short squalls of much needed rain.

'Fetch us a beer will you Jake; it's hot this evening,' Mary asked, as they sat on the front porch watching the students go by on bikes or roller boards, or in brightly painted jeeps.

'I'm out of here in a sec. I have a tennis lesson. Just wanted to hear what goes with the story, Dad,' he said when he returned with three cans of Bud Light.

'It's looking good. I have talked to my literary agent

and she seems keen on the idea. I have asked for an upfront fee to cover travel to Europe. We will soon find out. Not much else yet, except I have written the first section.'

'And what of the yacht? Did you fax our man in Egypt? Not that we need to now we are back – though it would be polite,' said Mary, as an afterthought.

'Hey, hold on a minute Mom: of course we do. If Dad writes a great book the film people will want to buy the yacht for the "up close and personal" scenes. We should buy her ourselves, if the price is right. It makes sense.'

'That's not a bad idea,' Alex pondered, 'but I have some work to do first; though I will contact the Yacht Agency to keep them on their toes.'

'You two need to come down to earth. Since our holiday you have been in another world. If, and knowing your father that is a big "if", this book gets finished then we can see if *Carina* is still an option.'

'There you go again … I'm off. See you later,' said Jake before collecting his bike from the side of the house and cycling away, carrying a tennis racquet over his shoulder.

Alex looked intently at Mary as he sipped his beer, thinking she was not bad for almost forty-five, but a little too sharp with him at times.

'I have more news,' Alex told her. 'This morning I talked to a Mrs Barbara Delrose in England. She and her husband owned *Carina* for many years; after the Royals. She would not give me any details over the phone, but has asked me to visit.'

'Oh. When would you plan to fly? You have only just got home.'

'As soon as possible. I am ready to go with this story and don't want anyone else to beat me to it. Would next month be OK? This would give me time to write up my notes so far.'

After a few moments in thought Mary said, 'Well, Jake is back at school and I am back at work, so you won't be missed *too* much.' Then she stood up and walked behind Alex, putting her arms around his shoulders.

'That wasn't very kind of me. I know that once you have a bee in your bonnet there's no stopping you. All I ask is that you take care and keep me updated: and hurry home.'

'Great. Let's celebrate with one of my pasta specials and a bottle of Chianti,' Alex suggested. 'Why don't you sit comfortably on the terrace and enjoy the evening. I'll call you when I have everything under control.'

Mary followed him through house. She had collected Victorian antiques for years, attending auction sales and avidly following personal adverts in *The Record*, their local paper. The pine dresser, side tables and bookcase mixed easily with the mahogany grandfather clock and cabinets. Hand-hooked rugs on heart-pine floors filled the spaces between the wide high-backed armchairs and deep cushioned settees. These formed three sides of a square facing the pine fireplace with marble hearth. Lace curtains were looped inside folding shutters, affording protection from the hot sunshine. The high ceilings also helped to keep the sitting areas cool, and the wide oak beams had brass and glass lanterns hanging between; an old softer style of lighting, which she preferred to modern spots.

The swing-seat was her favourite place in the garden, a better noun than 'yard'; much more in keeping with the wide borders she had planted with a mixture of local plants and roses. Three citrus trees ringed by oleander and hibiscus bushes offered patches of shade on the small lawn, and wisteria covered the white fencing behind. The house stood on raised piers to protect from flooding and to give air circulation and was built of clapboard. It had once been a brick building, but had been partly demolished after a fire and rebuilt on the same footprint in the early 1900s. The original slate tiles had cracked with the sun's heat and been replaced by the local cypress-shaker shingles.

'This is a dream house, and I should be happy,' she thought. 'Yet somehow things are not as they should be. I really wish I had a husband with a regular job. Maybe then we would be able to spend more quality time together. Things have really cooled off between us recently. Not good!'

Seven

Deep winter was early, arriving a month before Christmas, covering the whole of England with a thick white blanket of snow. Delighted children in bright-coloured pompom hats ran about shouting with glee at this unexpected holiday from school; exchanging snowballs and building snowmen, unaware of the transport and power chaos these conditions caused. England had never been sufficiently equipped to cope with severe weather.

Luckily, Alex had arrived in London the day before the heaviest snowfall and was able to drive south before the roads became blocked. He made good use of the satellite navigation system in the hired Hyundai and found his way from the M3 motorway onto the M27 and then south at Cadnam Corner to Lyndhurst. Here, he found a parking spot outside Kate's Café and stopped for a much-needed bowl of beef soup, followed by a mug of coffee and a slice of homemade chocolate cake, before heading onto a minor road to Beaulieu.

Before leaving the States, Alex had looked up the New Forest on the Internet, so was not surprised to see wild ponies, a donkey or two, and cattle roaming freely amongst the monster oak trees that lined the winding lanes. This ancient pasture-woodland was created in 1079 by William the Conqueror as a park for deer hunting and had recently been designated a National Park; the largest unenclosed area in southern England. As he approached Beaulieu the skies darkened, the roads became very dicey and small ice flakes brushed his windscreen.

'You have arrived,' decided the bossy voice of the Satnav, and Alex slowed and glanced around. A small wooden sign on his right pointed to Brook Street and as he turned into the lane he spied a wicket fence and gate enclosing the gardens of his destination – Rose Cottage. Having parked he walked under the lattice rose bower and down the bricked pathway to the front of the home and tapped the imp knocker.

To his surprise, the door was answered almost instantly by a smiling old lady dressed in a fur-trimmed cloak with hood, and leather boots.

'Alex?' she asked, 'please call me Barbara, welcome,' adding as they shook hands, 'I thought, as you have been travelling for two days, you may appreciate a walk around our village before dark. Can I lend you an overcoat?'

'That would be very welcome,' he said (attempting an English accent) and shrugged into the generous camel hair three-quarter length British Warm that she offered.

It was snowing more heavily and, as is often the case in winter, the evening was very still: hooting owls, lapping river water and the crunch of their feet on the crisp ground the only sounds as the sky darkened.

'It is a little colder here than where you come from, isn't it?' Barbara asked.

'Yes, but most invigorating after the Florida humidity,' Alex reassured her. 'Thank you for suggesting the visit.'

As they walked towards the village, along the flint walls and metal gates guarding Palace House, Barbara told him how King John had bestowed the land to the Cistercian monks in 1202 and their ancient Abbey still stands on the estate. The Lord of the Manor now runs the National Motor Museum in the grounds, which is a major attraction for thousands of tourists in the summer months. The terraced brick cottages they passed served the dual purpose of craft shops and homes and were lit by old-style street lanterns. They could see the glowing sign for the Beaulieu Arms as they carefully walked up the slippery incline of Palace Lane, alongside the river.

'Let's go into the Arms to tell them you have arrived and will be back later to move into your room and have supper,' Barbara suggested.

'Yes, good idea, I was wondering where you had booked,' Alex replied.

An open log fire roared in the entrance hall opposite the reception desk, and the subtle lighting and warmth of the greeting they received from the manager made them aware of how very cold it had become outside.

'We won't stop now,' Barbara told him, 'but will be back for supper at about seven o'clock, if you could tell the chef. There will be three of us.'

They retraced their steps and were soon sitting in armchairs in front of Barbara's own blazing fire, warming their hands and feet.

'This is certainly a haven of peace and tranquillity, Barbara,' Alex said, having studied the old mahogany clocks, brass fittings and Georgian furniture. 'But do you have plenty to do here in winter?'

'Oh no,' she was quick to say, 'like many of my neighbours who have homes all along the east bank of the Beaulieu River, I only come down to Rose Cottage on occasional weekends in the winter. Mostly I live in London, and then spend three or four months here in the summer.'

What a pity, Alex thought, that so many beautiful homes all over the world are left empty for months on end. His faith in Barbara was soon restored, however.

'A couple who work at the museum in the summer live here in winter, rent free, to care for the cottage; keep it dry and warm and do some weeding when the weather is good. They are staying with their daughter this weekend.'

There was a bang as the front door closed, and the

sound of shuffling in the hall before an elderly, red-nosed gentleman entered the living room, rubbing his hands.

'What a drive. There were a number of accidents on the black ice,' he said, blowing on his hands. 'I have only been into the Lyndhurst office as I did not want to risk being too far from home tonight. How do you do? David Pope, Barbara's companion,' he explained.

'This is Alex, the American author I was telling you about. He is interested in *Babs*, or *Carina* as she has been renamed, and our times on board. We have just returned from a short walk, and I had planned to tell him how you found the boat for us. Now you can relate the start of the story and I will tell Alex the rest. Let me fetch a pot of tea first to warm us up.'

As Barbara filled three Poole Pottery mugs from a flower-power teapot Alex admired her fading beauty. She must be almost seventy, he thought, yet with her slim figure, pale blue eyes surrounded by smile lines, her slightly upturned nose, heart-shaped face with pale curls falling onto her forehead and firm chin, she seemed to be younger and stronger than he had expected. She nodded lovingly at David to begin.

'I suppose I was the one to start it all. My family had been in the antique business for over 100 years and I took control of the business after the war. In the fifties I spent a great deal of time in Germany and France collecting items to bring back to England, and one of my customers was Princess Margaret. When she was in Germany, I would often escort her to parties or to the opera and was asked to cruise on their yacht on a number of occasions. One summer there was a party on board to celebrate the re-naming of *Carina* to *Prince Charles* and I was invited by the Princess to attend. The captain told me then that the yacht would be coming on the market and later contacted me with the details. I immediately rang to tell Keith Delrose, Barbara's fiancé, and he was very interested.'

Barbara interrupted: 'Didn't you go with Keith to negotiate the purchase and bring her across the Channel, David? I never heard the details as it was just before our wedding.'

'Yes, I rang Keith to tell him I could highly recommend this boat. At ninety feet she would fit perfectly on his river mooring and had been well maintained for high days and holidays cruising on the Rhine and inland waterways of Europe. I told him that she was expensively equipped and comfortable and would be just the base he needed for his racing weekends.' He smiled at Barbara before adding, 'I also said that his gorgeous little lady would be overjoyed when she set eyes on his purchase. I agreed to go to Germany with him to deal with the agent for the Goëring family and after we had stocked up in Hamburg we motored her home, full speed ahead, with no problems.'

'You devils kept all of this from me,' Barbara said, 'and it was not until Keith and I returned from a party in the Isle of Wight that I realized why you had both been so secretive.'

Barbara then told Alex that she had been working in Sotheby's in London, sharing an apartment with a cousin, when she had met Keith at an auction. After only knowing each other for a month they had to admit that they were deeply in love. Her father had died shortly afterwards leaving her Rose Cottage in his will. Keith had been very much the 'ladies' man', enjoying a busy social life in London, where he ran a printing firm, and spending his weekends and holidays skiing in winter and racing power boats in summer. He was almost thirty, and had been thinking that it was high time he looked for a wife and started planning for family life.

'To be quite truthful', she added wistfully, 'I believe it

was after he helped me move into this cottage, and saw the river frontage and mooring, that he began to think in terms of pooling our resources!'

'Anyway, this particular warm spring day we were cruising back down the Beaulieu River and I was looking through my binoculars at the birds nesting in the reeds and other river wildlife when we approached a shiny white hull with *Babs* painted on the transom. I shrieked with delight and asked Keith if he could believe that someone had a boat with my nickname. The penny dropped when I caught him laughing and steering up towards the long, sleek vessel with a canvas canopy shading the aft deck.'

'He tied up alongside and helped me on board, gave me a huge hug and hurled me around.' I yelled 'Hey, put me down you brute and give me some answers. Is this our yacht? Why didn't you tell me?'

He answered my queries by bowing low in knightly fashion and asking if I liked my wedding present. He confessed that he should have waited until after our wedding but was too impatient. After curtsying, holding out the sides of my shorts, I asked him to take me on the grand tour so that I could make up my mind.

'Lead on kind sir.'

Hand in hand we walked the decks, peered into every cubby hole, and admired the gleaming varnish. Keith would have carried me over the threshold but the steps down into the saloon were rather narrow. I followed him and admired the elegant room before seeing the gift-wrapped box, with a huge pink bow, on the table; and a basket of roses on the sideboard.

'Oh my darling, what a wonderful surprise! You spoil me. How on earth did you manage to carry these roses on board without them blowing everywhere?'

I hadn't realised before how thoughtful Keith could be. He lifted my hand and gently kissed it before handing me a pair of scissors. I ripped off the wrapping, impatient to discover the contents of the box, and lifted out a square metal object, asking, 'Is it a toaster?'

'No, the new portable record player; specially made for 45s – and ladies who spend a great deal of time sunbathing on the deck of their boats. Look in the bottom of the box.'

I delved down and removed a small packet of records and read the labels – 'Wonderful World' by Sam Cook; 'Stuck on You', 'It's Now or Never' and 'Are you Lonesome Tonight?' by Elvis Presley; 'Tonight's the Night' by the Shirells; 'There is Something on my Mind' by Bobby Marchan, and wondered.

'What exactly do *you* have in mind, my love?' I asked, snuggling up to him.

Ignoring my question he told me that while in Germany to collect the yacht he saw a floor show featuring Roy Orbison who sang 'Only the Lonely'. This made Keith realise how much he missed me. Apparently Orbison sang partly in German, which was very touching and much appreciated by the audience.

'So I bought his record and others, and thought the battery player would be useful on the boat,' and he slipped 'Stuck on You' in the slot, took me in his arms, and we danced round and round the table as I told him that I had been lonely too. He brushed back my hair and whispered in my ear that he had all kinds of things on his mind; but I firmly pointed out that it was only two o'clock in the afternoon and I was dying to view the rest of the boat.'

'Fine, we have all the time in the world ... that is before our dinner date.'

I studied the silk curtains, the green leather chairs and bench seat, the ornate table, the ornaments, paintings and rugs and told him that I liked the layout. Then I told him how clever he was to buy such an elegant yacht, with such classic lines, and that apart from the engine room (as I had not brought my overalls) I wanted to see everything. He bundled the wrapping paper into a ball and placed the records and player on the side and then lifted me up to sit on the table. Standing back and looking at me he said something rather romantic like 'I adore your layout and your classic lines. At the moment I am not at all interested in the boat, only you. You could easily change your outfit in the owners' cabin … collecting a tub of chocolate ice cream from the galley first.'

Only a week before our marriage, so what the heck, I thought. But ice cream?

Luckily it was a hot day: perfect for finding out what a pleasure it is to be painted with chocolate and then licked all over. I was a lollypop and Easter egg rolled into one. Back in the early sixties 'gentle folk' attempted to 'save themselves' for their wedding night but over the previous months I had been tempted many times to give in to Keith's amorous advances.

'From our first date I had known that Keith was the one. He had watched my every move, devouring me with his deep brown eyes, when we met as arranged in the theatre auditorium. His large hands had gently bumped mine as we found our seats, and this shock of knowing enthralled me. As I encountered his strong, wilful character, and listened to his deep sexy voice, I found myself wanting to know everything about him.

'Keith, maybe knowing this, played a canny game. We became friends first: laughing at each other's jokes, learning each other's foibles and sharing past experiences and family reminiscences. Each time we met it was with restrained pleasure that we pecked each other on the cheek; each time we parted we took care not to show our deep regret that our time together had ended so quickly.

Neither mentioned how lonely they felt when apart, or how they counted the minutes to the next encounter; but we knew. It must have been this way for over three months, and I was wondering if I had been mistaken, when we were invited to a birthday party on a Thames boat with many mutual acquaintances. The wine, the music, the fun of this balmy evening on the river was too much. We sat together on the poop deck and Keith took me into his arms and told me how much he loved me.

'We found an empty cabin, almost falling down the narrow curving staircase, and stood close together in the gloomy interior, our hearts thumping in unison, enjoying the privacy and excitement. It was then that I knew we should go no further and pushed Keith away. "Let's wait," I whispered. "We have years ahead of us – and I would like to be a virgin on our wedding day." So, holding hands, we climbed back onto the deck and joined the party. It was a week before our marriage, on *Babs*, that I did give in – with no regrets.'

Back in the present Barbara watched as David threw another log on the fire. 'We had twelve good years. With a part-time crew, and David's help whenever he could join us, we travelled far and wide,' she said, and handed Alex a blue album before balancing on the arm of his chair to describe the places depicted in the photos. 'We laid up the yacht every winter, in the Hamble yard, and launched her every spring. Weekends were spent cruising along the British coast – east to Chichester, Brighton and Hastings and west to Torquay and Dartmouth.'

'My favourite memories are of diving to pick up lobsters and crabs in the Channel Islands, and visiting the Casino in Cherbourg, France. I cleaned up 450 Francs on our first visit!' said David.

'And I won't tell what happened on the second...' Barbara said dreamily. 'We would leave the mooring late on Fridays and have an overnight crossing of the Channel; arriving in France at dawn. If Keith and David were racing we would tow the Cigar boat behind.'

'You certainly visited some beautiful places; Dauville, St Malo, Honfleur … isn't that where the artists gathered at the turn of the century?' Alex asked.

'Yes, indeed. The town is full of galleries and the boys had to drag me away when it was time to leave,' she said. 'Tell Alex the story of the Paris race, David.'

'Let me see, that was for the Six Hour Race – it was a long time ago. We needed a week's holiday for that trip. It took us two days to navigate the twists and turns of the Seine. The river was tidal to Rouen and then locked above, and there was a five-knot speed limit. When we reached the centre of Paris we moored alongside the river bank under the Eiffel Tower; couldn't have been more central for that was where the race started and finished.'

'The crew and I spent hours on deck checking the fenders as we shook up and down with the wake of the procession of barges ploughing the river. And when the race started the noise was overwhelming,' Barbara remembered.

'Was there enough width for racing in the Seine?' Alex wanted to know.

'Just. The race was round the Île de la Cité and six other islands … and round, and round, and round. We were asked to race an Italian designed Molinari Cat, which by today's standards, could be called a fast outboard runabout. I for one was very glad to finish.'

Alex took advantage of the short silence, which followed their memories. 'A few years ago I took my son to watch a race in Sarasota Harbor in Florida and we saw the American development of that boat – the *Maltese Magnum* it was called. Phew!

Barbara told them that talking of hot boats always made

her thirsty before asking David to fetch a cold bottle of wine. 'Then I can tell you the best part of that trip for me', she said. He soon returned with an ice bucket holding a bottle of Chablis, removed the cork and poured out three glasses which they clinked together calling 'Cheers!'

'Thank you,' said Barbara. 'Well, following the race we attended the prize giving dinner which was held in the Eiffel Tower Restaurant; climbing right to the top although the men were very dizzy from the race...'

David butted in, '...and who would greet us, while we were getting our breath back, but the race organizer...'

It was Barbara's turn to interrupt: 'and guess what ... he asked us to look after the cabaret guest for the evening – the French singing star Sacha Distel. He was such fun and our table spent the evening swapping jokes and laughing rather loudly. Afterwards one lady, whose husband was a major competitor, asked me why the star had been seated with us...'

'...and Barbara told her that we had been friends for years! What else could she say?'

'You always tell the punch line to my stories. There are so many, and the sun was always shining. Anyway, the highlight of the summer was always the Cowes Week Regatta in August; and that was where we had our last boating adventure...'

The lady of the house settled down into the cushions of her chair and recalled that summer. It was the middle of the hot August of 1972 and their yacht was on a swinging mooring off Egypt Point, to the west of Cowes on the Isle of Wight. She had been sunbathing on the aft deck, with her record player by her side, anticipating the return of her husband from sea trials with his power boat. While waiting she leafed through a pile of magazines fresh from Keith's printing press and exclaimed as she read one article, folding down the page. Just then a deep-throated roar from twin outboards announced his arrival. He drove alongside, cut the engines and tied up to *Babs*. After clambering aboard and removing his red helmet he rushed over to join his wife, kissing her gently then giving her a bear hug.

'I have been waiting all day for that,' he told her, smiling. 'Let me remove this sweltering gear and I will be back with a drink.' When he returned he was in shorts and a T-shirt and carried two bottles of Coke. Barbara asked him how the boat had behaved, wondering why he had been away so long.

'We like the design changes and the engines are much more powerful after their tune-up. There's hope for tomorrow. You look great in that swimsuit by the way.'

'Thanks. I chose the colour to match your speedster. I'm thrilled that you like it.'

'It's not really the suit I am admiring, but what's in it!' he told her.

'So you still fancy me, after all these years?'

'More than you will ever know. But enough of that talk. What have you been up to?'

'I have been looking forward to telling you … while I was reviewing these art magazines you print, I found a fascinating piece that could be of great interest to us. Apparently there are still many paintings that were lost during the war years and have yet to be traced. Goëring often journeyed in his own train, and purloined art works from galleries and private homes as he travelled.'

Keith nodded. 'Yes I heard that many stolen artifacts were retrieved from his hunting lodge and home.'

'I was wondering if he could have brought some paintings on board his yacht, along with all the other priceless possessions that we have had to stow. We may have missed some secret locker.'

Keith suggested that they would have been found by now, but promised to search from stem to stern – after the race. Barbara sat on his lap, wrapped her arms round his shoulders and told him how good he was.

'I could stay here for hours, but I must go and dress ... it is getting cool. Be back soon,' she told him.

Keith relaxed, leaning back in his chair, with his hands behind his head, watching the sailboats returning to the marina after their day's racing. When his wife returned she was in a more serious mood.

'I have been thinking ... watching all the smart modern yachts that have cruised past this afternoon ... could we think about building a new boat with all mod cons? If we have faster engines and more fuel and water capacity we could venture further. Even across the Bay of Biscay and down to the Med. You won't be racing forever and we could explore Portugal, Spain, Italy and all points east.'

'You are full of ideas this evening, my love. Let's get over tomorrow and we will consider our options. Good, here is David to join us. He must have taken the nanny boat,' Keith said, standing to greet his friend and pulling up a chair for him.

Barbara smiled at David and welcomed him on board before asking him to join them for supper (which she was just about to prepare) and whether he would like a drink.

'Let me get my own drink,' David replied, following Barbara to the galley and returning to sit with David to watch as the sun sank below the horizon and lights glowed all around them. Speaking softly, Keith confided:

'She hasn't said as much, but I think Barbara would like me to give up racing. She has been asking if we could have a modern yacht for cruising. I must say my thoughts have been turning the same way.'

'Do you really want to sell this yacht, Keith?' his friend replied. 'You will laugh, but I have had a secret code for the boat for quite a while. B is for 'bloody hell' when I bump my head on the low bulkheads; A is for '——' when I have to hand-pump the bilges; B is for 'bitch' when the engines falter; S is for '—' when the packing on the A-brackets is leaking – *Babs*! Don't you dare tell Barbara.' They both found this very funny.

Later that evening crowds gathered all along the promenade between Cowes and Egypt Point. The street lights, the floodlights on the old church steeple and the Royal Yacht Squadron Tower were reflected in the rippling sea. Boats of all shapes and sizes fill every space in the sea. Everyone is waiting for the famous end-of-regatta-week firework display.

Keith and David leant against the rail watching the activity onshore and the juggling of boats all around them.

'What a lovely evening for the fireworks,' David said. 'I hope the weather is as calm tomorrow.'

'Me too. Don't tell Barbara. If the weather forecast is bad, she will worry. She is always telling me that she does not want to be a young widow.'

At that moment Barbara joined them and asked what they were talking about; hoping that they were not keeping secrets. Keith was just about to tell her when there was a loud explosion and a shower of multi-coloured stars filled the sky. They sat back on the deck and watched the display in wonder. The noises of shouting and clapping, oohs and aahs, and the counting of the explosions followed by silver tracers, reached them from the shore. They joined in.

An early morning mist dampened the boat deck and a low fog concealed the harbour and distant coastline. Despite limited visibility, race boats zoomed here and there, crossing each other's wakes creating turbulence and noise. Wrapped in her foul-weather gear Barbara sat dejectedly on the forepeak warming her hands on a steaming mug of coffee. Keith and David joined her wearing tight white jump-suits and carrying red helmets. They each gave her a hug and Keith asked her to wish them luck.

'It looks good,' he told her. 'This will soon clear. It is often the harbinger of a brilliant day. Don't catch cold sitting out here in the damp; there is an hour before the race is due to start.'

'Just you take care. We will celebrate with a steak on the grill when you win,' she said, and rushed over to give her husband another hug. Releasing him with reluctance she watched them climb into their race boat and speed away, giving cheery waves.

After clearing away their breakfast dishes and taking a hot shower Barbara returned to her forward viewing spot with binoculars. A wall of spray in the distance, growing ever higher, alerted her to the imminent racing start. As the starter's gun thundered, a line of powerful hulls pointed towards her. Soon they had passed the corral of moored boats, which pitched and tossed like wild horses. Engines roared and surged.

As she watched, the lead boat suddenly peeled off to the left, causing panic with those following, and headed straight up the steep pebbled beach. It came to an abrupt splintering halt. Barbara gave a horrified gasp and stared at the scene. It slowly dawned on her that Keith's boat had been part of a terrible collision and she collapsed on the deck, sobbing quietly.

Barbara wiped her eyes as she came to the end of her story and Alex looked at her with some concern. 'What a tragic story,' he said and was tempted to tell her of the loss of his own family. He decided that it was not a good idea, at the same time realizing that he needed someone to listen to his outpourings, much as Barbara had.

Looking at David she replied, 'Luckily, David was thrown clear. After he healed he set about putting me together again ... such a support through all the years. Now we are old ... older ... there are so many memories to share.'

'More than that – our lives,' said David. 'Listen, we have been following the adventures of *Carina* – as she is now called – ever since we sold her and she returned to Hamburg.'

'Did she go home? I hadn't known that,' Alex mused.

'Yes. The man who bought her was the infamous German reporter, Gerd Heidemann of the *Hitler Diaries* scam. Did you hear about this scandal in America?'

'Vaguely, but go on...'

'May I interrupt you for a moment?' Barbara asked us. 'It is almost time for us to walk up to the Arms for supper; I booked a table for seven o'clock. We can continue our reminiscences over a steak and kidney pie.'

'Good idea,' the men replied, in unison.

'The supper is on me,' promised Alex.

They dressed warmly in coats, gloves, hats and scarves and walked briskly along the snowy path to Beaulieu. Barbara was carrying a large string bag, which Alex offered to carry only to be refused. After hanging their gear on the Victorian hat stand in the hotel lobby they were shown to a table in the elegant restaurant, overlooking the icy Beaulieu River.

'Hey, you folks,' said Alex as they sat in plush arm chairs, 'you told me we were going to the pub. This is more like a five-star Manor House. If I had known I would have suggested that we go Dutch!' adding quickly, 'Only joking.'

'I thought this would be nearer, and better than the Crown and you do have a room here for the night,' Barbara explained.

'Wait until you hear what we have for you. You won't regret treating us to supper, I promise,' David told him.

'Does this have anything to do with Heidemann?'

'Sort of,' said Barbara, 'You see *Carina* was right at the centre of the whole episode. If Heidemann had not bought the boat he would have avoided the huge debts that led him to his involvement with criminals, sharks and spies...'

David butted in. 'It is a very involved story and best studied at home. So, we have a book for you relating the whole drama in detail; and a TV drama series that clarifies things.'

He handed the string bag to Alex, who peered inside and thanked them for all their trouble.

'Maybe I will not need to try and meet the man himself?' he wondered.

'I very much doubt whether you will hear anything from him, but it is worth a try. At least you will be able to judge for yourself the nature of the man. Apparently, he is still deep in debt and fed up to the teeth with all the nosey reporters; oh, and still denying any knowledge of the fraud.'

Alex told them that he was planning to fly to Hamburg the next day, if there were no flight problems due to the snow conditions, and would be leaving Hampshire in the morning.

In a hushed voice Barbara warned him to take care wherever he travelled. 'The Secret Services in both East and West Germany now claim that he worked for them for many years, even after his time in jail. Before I forget I would like to ask a favour – if you have a chance would you ask him if he heard of any valuable paintings being hidden on *Carina* by Goëring.'

Alex said he would try. The waiter arrived with pints of bitter beer and menus for them to study, and the subject changed to the difficult political and financial problems facing both of their countries.

Back in his room Alex quickly settled into his huge four-poster bed with the book he had been given; speed-reading the relevant chapters before his meeting with Heidemann. He made a note of the questions he would like to ask. Maybe he would get some answers? He turned on the television to check the weather forecast and pulled back the curtains to find the terraced garden glittering with moonshine on ice. It had stopped snowing and no further falls were predicted – all systems go, he told himself.

The last thoughts he had before falling into a profound sleep were of his wife and son. He must remember to ring them when he arrived in Hamburg.

Eight

Having lived all of his forty-nine years in the United States, never venturing abroad, Alex was becoming a seasoned world traveller. He had visited Switzerland and Egypt in the spring and now he was making a fist of negotiating the narrow lanes and motorways of England with a right-hand drive hire car in deep mid-winter; needing to arrive at Heathrow Airport in plenty of time for his next adventure. He had surprised himself at his ability to stay calm and not display his nervous excitement. Good preparation is the key he kept telling himself.

He had spent some time viewing photos, maps and tourist information on his Sony Vaio before leaving the Beaulieu Hotel, and had booked a room at the Hamburg Mövenpick Hotel online; using a discount membership card given to him by the hotel manager in El Gouna. After their wonderful stay in Egypt he felt confident with the facilities and service offered by this Swiss chain of hotels. Situated just over a mile from all the places of interest in the large and sprawling city centre he was prepared for a walk to his rendezvous.

Much of old Hamburg had been destroyed by fire in 1842 and half of her buildings destroyed by the Allied bombings at the end of World War II. It had taken twenty years to rebuild the city, the major port and the second largest city in Germany after Berlin. Being on the confluence of the rivers Alsler and Bille with the Elbe, forming two lakes, the garden city was said to be a giant Venice with many bridges over canals. Wharfs for cargo ships, old factory buildings and rebuilt churches were the subject of the tourist photographs.

The flight from London took just over an hour, and visibility was good, so Alex was able to view the industrial sprawl, docklands, parks and city buildings to complete his imaginary picture. He had decided to take the airport shuttle to the main railway station and the metro to the Sternschanze stop – one hundred metres from his hotel. He would use a taxi on the return journey and maybe later that night.

By seven o'clock Alex was sitting at a long table in the Groninger Braukeller, Ost-West Strasse, sipping a stein of beer. All around him people were singing and swinging along with the Tyrol band playing mountain music. The aroma of malt and hops hung in the air, and huge brass vats with copper piping lined the beer hall. A group of young students with college scarves filled the empty spaces on the benches each side. After ordering drinks from waitresses in low-cut lacey blouses they joined in the songs; linked arms with him and swayed from side to side.

One student shouted in his ear, asking where he had come from. 'You are not local, are you?' he asked.

'No,' Alex shouted back. 'I am from the USA.'

The other students heard this above the noise of the band and stopped singing to turn their full attention on Alex whilst tapping out the beat and clapping.

'What is a Yank doing here, on his own?' one student asked him, pushing her blond fringe back behind her ears.

Alex looked at his watch before answering, 'I am waiting for a friend. He will be here soon.'

As these words left his mouth the doors flew open and a tired old man entered. He took off his woolly hat to reveal a bald head and hung his coat, scarf, and hat on a hook by the door. He wiped his glasses on his sweatshirt as he peered around the beer hall. He looks older than his seventy-five years, thought Alex, with dark rings under his eyes, stubble (definitely not of the 'designer' variety) and bowed shoulders.

Alex stood up, leaving gaping students, and went over to greet Gerd Heidemann. Behind he could hear the young laughing and jeering.

'You are Mr Johnson? I hope I am not late.'

'Call me Alex ... no, you made good time. I have only been here a few minutes.'

'There is a quiet table over there, in the alcove, where we can hear ourselves think,' Gerd said, leading him by the elbow. 'As you see, I am not popular with the people here. In spite of them, it was a good place for us to meet as it is not far from my home.'

They sat down at a small corner table and the waiter arrived with menus and took a small black object from his waistcoat pocket. Alex watched the waiter as he stuck a Hitler moustache to his top lip, snapped his heels together and extended his arm.

'Kurt, that is no longer funny,' Gerd admonished; while Alex, who was finding the scene very embarrassing, glanced around and was relieved to find no one was watching.

'All the tourists enjoy the cabaret, I expect. We will have two steins of beer and your best beef steak and chips please, medium rare for me. With salad, Gerd?'

'It will come with the order. Rare for me please, Kurt.'

The waiter pulled their beer from a nearby vat tap and handed Alex a pad and pen, telling him that the students were asking for his autograph. As he obliged the band played *The Star Spangled Banner* and there was much bowing and scraping in their direction by the conductor.

'Why me?' Alex asked the waiter.

'They say that anyone meeting with the great spy Heidemann must be famous.'

'Tell them to stop fooling around and leave us alone,' an angry Gerd spluttered as the waiter shrugged and left with a wide grin on his face.

'I expect you have to put up with this wherever you go,' said Alex sympathetically.

'For years. The press will not drop the stories. They love to speculate. Especially now the Stazi have released my files.'

'You told me on the telephone that you would not talk to me about their accusations, only *Carina*.'

'I was angry … too many strange calls. People banging on my door at all times of the day and night … but you must know that the wretched boat, the diaries and the Secret Service are all intertwined. Cannot be separated. How I wish that I had never heard of Goëring's yacht. It was a black hole into which I poured many thousands of marks. Don't think of buying her … every owner has been doomed.'

Alex replied, 'My plan was to write about the boat's adventures over seven vastly different decades; a sort of yachting version of *The Yellow Rolls-Royce* – did you ever see that film?'

'Yes, yes. As I said before … as with that story it will not be possible to write about the boat without the owners and their exploits. It seems to me that they have all suffered. For me it was the worst. You see, I was duped … I was just a scapegoat. I will tell you what I can and you must make up your own mind about the rest.'

Alex placed his small recorder on the table and switched it on. He had hoped that Gerd would concentrate on *Carina*, as there was not much written about his times on board, but he seemed ready to tell his life story. It was to take a long time.

* * *

'It was in the winter of 1973 that I found the yacht in Bonn. The price was high: 160,000 DMs so I had to mortgage my house to buy her. A friend of mine, Axel Thomsen, was an engineer and helped me sail her back to Hamburg on the inland waterways with only one functional engine. At the Hamburg shipyards we watched as she was hauled clear of the water and put into dry dock. The yard manager walked round the boat with me and I asked him to check the hull to make sure she was watertight, have his engineer service the engines and his electrician quote to update the electrical systems. The interior modernisation would follow.

'He told me that the engines would need a complete overhaul but it would be preferable if we replaced them with modern Mercedes diesels. Either way the old ones would have to come out.'

'I asked if the cost of the engines would be reflected in the resale value and he wondered why I would be thinking of selling: I had just purchased her. I didn't tell him then but I was already thinking I could do enough refurbishment to enhance the price and make a profit. I was in financial difficulties after the end of my third marriage and Axel lent me some money to have her made watertight. Word soon spread that I was not able to restore her and the next year, with the yard clamouring for money, I moved her to the Hamburg Marina putting their expensive quotes for re-panelling the stateroom, re-corking the decks and fibre-glassing the hull to protect the wood, on hold.'

The waiter arrived with their oval platters of steak and chips with a side salad. Gerd was hungry and dug straight into his steak with a long sharp-tooth steak knife, then loaded his mouth with fries. Alex, very tired after travelling all day, felt slightly queasy as he studied ten ounces of red meat, wondering where to start.

'Do you think that we could continue our discussion tomorrow, Gerd? There is so much to talk about and I am rather bushed. You could meet me at my hotel; there is a lounge/library where we can talk privately in the morning. I am staying for three days so we have time.'

'If you will pay my taxi fare,' Gerd told him, looking embarrassed. This agreed they finished their supper to the increasingly noisy drums in the background. It was becoming almost impossible to take part in a conversation, and they were both happy to escape from the ale house and walk along the icy pavements towards the town centre.

The small meeting room at the Mövenpick Hotel was empty when Alex arrived at ten o'clock the next morning to wait for Heidemann. A short, fat waitress bustled in with the tray of coffee and biscuits that had been ordered, lit the electric flame-fire, and turned on the Tiffany lights overhanging the coffee tables. Alex looked along the shelves of books that formed a library on two sides of the lounge, but finding nothing of interest he sank into one of the cherry red overstuffed arm chairs and tried hard to understand a German newspaper.

It was just past eleven when Gerd finally joined him and was ready to continue his story. He seemed to be a touch more reserved than the previous evening, glancing about as if checking for eavesdroppers and somewhat disconcerted when the recorder was switched on. However, he soon settled down in the warmth and comfort of his seat to continue the story.

'As I was saying I was in debt to the yard by this time; unwisely I had asked them to totally redecorate the boat and re-panel the stateroom, so I found it necessary to visit my bank manager. I gave him a copy of all the bills associated with *Carina* and explained how I planned to sell the boat when the work was finished. I needed 160,000 DMs. He was kind and said he would talk to their loans officer, but may not be able to accommodate me; even when he heard of the scoops I was working on for Stern. I had been a star reporter for them for several years. I left the bank feeling depressed but quickly cheered up when Edda reminded me of the party we had planned on *Carina*, the following weekend.

'I met Edda, the beautiful daughter of Hermann and Emma Goëring, when I started to research the history of their yacht. She was unmarried and devoted to the memory of her father. We became attracted to each other. Through her contacts I was drawn into the circle of former Nazis who loved to visit us to drink our whisky and talk of former times. She gave me many of her momentos to adorn the yacht and I acquired others. *Carina* was developing into a shrine to Goëring and I had a wonderful idea. What if I taped the long reminiscences of our important guests for a book.

'I asked our Stern publisher, Nannen, to the party and he was very impressed with the boat and my idea. After some haggling, we did a deal. He offered me 60,000 DMs for this work and imposed no deadlines. Can you believe it? But this was to be paid in instalments and *Carina* was a bottomless pit. I still had debts.

'That summer Edda introduced me to her friend Gina who was a divorcee with two teenage daughters. We had much in common; both loving our times on *Carina* where we entertained survivors of Hitler's government and their families. We married and had a long honeymoon in South America, where we taped meetings with Nazi contacts for my book. That Christmas we held a big party. *Carina* was decorated with fairy lights above the wheelhouse and I booked a three-piece band to play on the aft deck. There must have been fifty guests that evening.

'Imagine my delight when, as I wandered around watching people chatting and drinking, I was approached by an elderly gentleman dressed in a white tuxedo and red bow tie; he was Fritz Steifel, a wealthy art dealer and collector of Nazi memorabilia (at that time against the law in Germany). I had met him before at an art auction. After the usual pleasantries I confided that I was in a spot of trouble and asked if he could help. "In what way?" he asked. I suggested a short-term loan from him could be paid back with money earned from all the important assignments I was undertaking for Stern.

'"With this extravagant lifestyle you are leading, I am not surprised," he said. "How much has the work on *Carina* cost so far?"

'"Far more than I had anticipated, Fritz. The yard has agreed to take stage payments and I was wondering if I could use *Carina* to display some of your old masterpieces and valuables. If I open the yacht as a museum I could pay you back."

'"That would take many years," he said. "You can certainly have some of my smaller pieces, but nothing of great value. Think of insurance costs ... and the worry."

'"I was downcast and he attempted to cheer me up by saying he would think things over and be in touch; then excused himself to talk to a lady client."

Alex interrupted his tale as Gerd's voice was dry and croaky, handing him a cup and asking:

'It seems to me that you were way over your head with debt and still spending money like water. Did you not worry that you would never be able to pay all these loans back?'

The situation sounded to Alex much like the present-day problems between mortgage holders and banks. After

Gerd had gulped down his coffee he said that the best was yet to come and continued.

'I was leaning over the rail on the jetty, staring moodily at the reflected lights, when I was joined by yet another man. This thin pale stranger asked whether I was the host, and I wondered if we had met before.

'"No. I work in an import/export business here in the Port. It was suggested to me that we should meet."

'"I have no interest in that business, I said, and was quick to tell him that I worked for Stern and travelled widely to cover scandals. He told me that he was well aware of my job and lifestyle and had been asked "by associates" to put a proposition to me. My heart rate shot up and beads of sweat jostled on my forehead. This could be the chance I have been waiting for. I thought, and tried to keep my voice calm as I asked what this was all about. Was it undercover work?

'"They are willing to pay well for any information you can find of the British and American Secret Service premises here in Germany," he told me. "Of particular interest is their military build-up and possible targets. You have been a reporter since 1953 so no one will question your delving into this. It is normally your way to shout about your projects to anyone who will listen, and some that won't; but not this time. You understand?"

'"So this is Secret Service work; I thought so. This is very dangerous for me – it would have to be very well paid," I told him, by way of acceptance.

'He explained that they had a carpenter in the Boat Yard who was working for his organisation and had been keeping me under surveillance. This man had fitted the mahogany panelling on *Carina*. When I had photos or information for them I should place them in the Goëring seat on the deck and hoist the German ensign. The carpenter would then collect the papers and leave a pay packet. How did this sound? I agreed to do what I could to find the details they asked for. I needed money and fast. All the man from the "import/export" company could say was "We know", before gliding down the gangplank and disappearing into the shadows.

'I drained my glass and was about to find a refill when another stranger approached and offered his hand.

'"Kurt Dobrow; good to meet you, Gerd," he said in a confidential manner and added, "I have heard all about you ... and I also taped that last conversation you had." He bent down and removed a small microphone from under the railing, holding it up under my nose in a menacing fashion. "That gentleman on the recording was from the East German Secret Service – Stasi as it is called." Once again I was damp with fear and pale under the neon lights on the jetty. This was all too much; staring at him through my misted horn-rimmed spectacles I managed to stutter:

'"Oh, this is news to me. I had never met him before."

'"Yet, from what I heard, you decided to do business with him. Shady business," was his stern retort.

'I tried to excuse myself by telling him about my financial worries and that I would do almost anything to cover my overwhelming debts. Ignoring my excuses he replied, to my surprise:

'"Good. I work for the West German Secret Service and also have a proposition for you. Every time you provide the other side with information you will give us a copy. For this I will pay double their offer. If you leave our copy in the same place, after lowering the flag, we will collect from there."

'Once again I promised to co-operate and asked him whether we would meet again.

'"Naturally. *Auf Wiedersehn,*" he replied and turned away, leaving the yacht unseen by the partying guests. I decided that it was high time I joined them. My life was becoming too complex; another double whisky may help.'

'So far,' Alex commented in a gentle tone, 'in addition to a salary for your daytime job, a loan from a friend, large debits at the bank and boatyard, down payments on an unwritten book, help from a business partner to start a museum on your yacht, you made lucrative deals with opposing spy networks. You were recently divorced and spending money like water on your new beau and an extravagant lifestyle: parties, travel, new homes, a new car and extensive renovation to your yacht; what we today call conspicuous consumption. Mad!'

'At times life became so crazy … I was crying one moment and laughing my head off the next. Listen … some weeks after the party I was working in the library of *Carina* with rain falling in sheets across the decks. I finished preparing a packet of notes and pictures for one set of spies, and ran along the deck under my umbrella to place it inside the Goëring seat. With difficulty, I fought wind and rain to raise the ensign.

'Back in the wheelhouse I watched a shady character slip along and collect. Excitedly I returned to the hiding place to find … nothing! No money. I put the second package in the seat and lowered the flag, before returning to shelter. As I watched, another dark figure hastily boarded the boat and removed my second package. Once more I returned to lift the lid … this time finding a wad of deuchmarks. The East Germans "forgot" and the West Germans kept their promise. Now wouldn't that make a hilarious scene in a comedy?'

Over a snack lunch in the hotel bar Gerd continued his *Carina* story, reminding Alex to first start his recorder. He was really enjoying the attention of a good audience and the hospitality of someone he considered to be of like mind.

'The following week I was typing at the saloon table surrounded by piles of books, photographs and papers when I heard the screech of tyres as a car draw up to the boat. Looking out I watched my visitor, Fritz Steifel, park his red convertible Mercedes by the boarding ramp and board carrying his briefcase. I welcomed him and excused my clutter, telling him that I was writing a big piece for Stern about the American troop and missile build up.

'He apologised with, "Sorry to disturb you, Gerd, but I have the most exciting news. Your troubles could be over." I told him that this was hard to believe. I couldn't wait to hear what he had to tell me. Carefully he took a black book out of his briefcase and put it on the table.

'"This is the scoop you have been waiting for. There, on the table, is a diary written by Hitler – in his own hand. I am told there are twenty-six other volumes. So far I have only bought one."

'I reverently picked up the book, studied the cover and turned the pages. Amazing. Of course, I wanted to know if it was genuine, as I had never heard even a rumour of such books. I wanted to show the work to my bosses at Stern, as I knew they would be fascinated. This could mean a big deal for them. Fritz agreed if I promised to be extra careful as the book was old, fragile and very valuable; which of course was obvious to me. My next question was about the dealer who sold such a diary, as I would like to make contact. Stern would want to check on his authenticity.

'After some obfuscation, Fritz finally admitted that there was no way that I could be introduced to the dealer. Had I ever heard of a plane crash in East Germany that destroyed all Hitler's private papers from his bunker? It seems, he told me, that the military official in charge of the wreckage stole the diaries and other important papers and smuggled them over the border to dealers in Stuttgart. If this was known that official would possibly be sentenced to death or life imprisonment.'

This seemed like a good moment to end the reminiscences for the day; so it was arranged that they would reconvene, same place same time, the following morning. Gerd, seemingly reluctant to return to his sparse lonely apartment, promised to be on time so that they could wrap up the interview before lunch, and have a hearty meal to celebrate. Alex repeated to him, before they wandered through the hall making for the double front doors, that he was mostly curious about Gerd's dealings on *Carina*, as the *Hitler Diaries* story was well documented; a suggestion he agreed to try hard to follow.

For the rest of the afternoon Alex listened to the recordings of Gerd's memories and made notes. There was certain irony in owning a prestigious yacht, originally designed and now restored in order to impress, only to have to break the law in order to maintain her: whatever Gerd did to try to plug the black hole of debt led to further financial and legal problems. That evening Alex gave these conundrums a rest, and to lighten his mood decided to walk to the State Opera House to enjoy Rossini's *The Barber of Seville* with the Australian Simone Young conducting. Alex awarded himself a good behaviour star for choosing a classic rather than the more raunchy shows he could have enjoyed. His life was changing. Later, as he prepared for bed, he looked in the bathroom mirror searching for any visible signs of his newly discovered international maturity, and detected a less harried countenance. It dawned on him that this was the first time for many years that he had been totally independent of the wishes and influences of 'significant others'. This freedom felt great. He did not ring home although it would be supper time in America.

Alex had time for a leisurely breakfast before meeting Gerd once again, and as they made themselves comfortable asked the question that had been pressing on his mind –

'Tell me, I must ask this for I have been reading about the *Hitler Diaries*; did you not wonder from the beginning whether you were being duped?'

'Of course; it was a priority to find out if they were genuine. I drove my old Volkswagen round to the Stern offices in high expectation that my colleagues would be as excited as I was. They dismissed my news as nonsense. The editor told me that no one believed my story because if they were genuine, they would have been discovered many years earlier, and told me not to pursue the story. He knew that I had many other leads to follow and described my attitude as over-zealous. Next I took the elevator to talk to my friend Tom Walder, who worked in the historical research department, to ask his opinion. While I waited patiently he studied the black book intently, and then roared with laughter.

'"If this is what you think it is we are into the *big time*," he said. "Together we must visit the top management if those guys downstairs won't take you seriously. Maybe with a financial enticement we could flush out the dealer. He won't be able to ignore a huge offer with conditions."

'Well, as you will have read, Manfred Fischer of Gruner and Jahr (Stern's parent corporation) was intrigued. He agreed that with twenty serialised volumes to work with Stern would make a fortune. Syndication deals worldwide would follow. He asked what sum was being asked for the full collection and I told him 85,000 DMs for each volume. I told him that there were conditions: the deal must be done in absolute secrecy. The dealer's brother, a General in the East German Army was involved. His life would be endangered if this leaked…'

Alex interrupted. 'He believed you?'

'Of course. He told me that he would take my word as far as authenticity was concerned as he trusted me. I was his top reporter. He planned, when the time was right to publish, to invite world experts to verify the origins of the diaries. As he took bundles of DMs from his wall safe, and placed them in my briefcase, he instructed me to deliver the next volumes to him personally.'

After slurping down a black coffee Gerd continued a story which still excited him.

'The next day I bought a new blue Volkswagen and drove to my yacht. As I parked a white van drove alongside. The driver, a jolly fellow with red cheeks and with short legs, jumped down and introduced himself as Konrad Kujau. As we boarded *Carina* he told me that he was the diary dealer and I almost fell off the gangplank. He must have heard of the money bait for he had changed his mind about dealing direct.

'Seated in the saloon with a brandy in front of him Konrad noted all the finery and asked:

'"You have a new car?"

'"Yes, about time. My old VW was falling apart. Let us talk business. I have news for you," I said.

'"Your paper wants to buy the diaries? Did you tell them it would be a slow process?"

'I told him that they had agreed to all his stipulations and that I had the first payment in my briefcase. He must contact his brother immediately to tell him that this deal was a matter of priority. He gulped down his drink and rose to leave; as he filled his own small case with the money he explained that he had work to do and people to see and hastily disembarked.'

Alex suggested that this should have been some indication

to Gerd that the dealer was shifty and not to be trusted. 'For two years you exchanged diaries for DMs with no serious questions asked; it seems incredible. Stern must have been losing patience.'

'Yes. The editor called an urgent meeting as they wanted to publish the diaries they had bought very soon. This was a defining moment. They had noticed that I was spending money like crazy on women, parties, cars, the yacht and holidays...'

'Wait,' Alex shouted. 'Were you paying down any of your huge debts with all the money you were now earning? It sounds as if your lavish lifestyle was causing suspicions, which eventually led to your downfall. You had large cash advances and the Stern management had spent hundreds of thousands buying up the manuscripts. Then you raised the price to over 200,000 DMs for each diary. Were you skimming?'

Gerd looked down at his scrawny hands, which were active in his lap, and did not answer but continued his monologue.

'I was in shock. I thought they should wait for the whole set; that would be a most exciting scoop, but first I wanted them to publish a book to wet the public's appetite. Now they had decided to accelerate the schedule. They had begun to contact rival news organizations in confidence. *Newsweek* and Murdoch's News Corporation were interested, and were sending their own experts to verify authenticity. Understandably, with 9 million DMs on the line, they hoped to recoup some of this outlay with sales. A further meeting was called for the next Tuesday. Tom and I felt hustled and returned to the yacht to drown our sorrows.

'The following weekend I arrived at the dock to find a young woman taking photos of *Carina*. I walked over and took her by the elbow, asking what she thought she was doing.

'"Hey, take your hands off me!" she cried. "If you are Monsieur Heidemann, and this is your yacht, I have every right to be here."

'"You had better come on board and tell me what this is all about," I said and led the way to the saloon. "Tell me why you were taking pictures of my yacht," I asked, "do you know someone who wants to buy her?"

'She sat down on the settee, admiring the green leather and removing the camera strap from around her neck. "Ah, non. I am a reporter with *Paris Match* and have just read an incredible press release. You are a star!"

'I asked her to relate all she knew, and pretended to be amazed to hear her news. Two independent experts had studied the black books, thought to be Hitler's handwritten diaries, and had determined that they were genuine. I had been nervously awaiting this information for days; sleeping poorly and drinking far too much.

'I asked the names of the two experts and was told that one was Hugh Trevor-Roper the Hitler historian and the other Gerhard Weinberg, from the University of North Carolina, for *Newsweek*. She told me that Trevor-Roper had been sceptical at first but the sheer volume of the diaries, covering thirty-five years, together with the paintings and drawings in them had convinced him that they were real. Weinberg had thought it significant that Hitler's signature was on every page; too much of a risk for a forger.

'It was the moment for celebration. I found a bottle of chilled Champagne, lifted down two of my best crystal glasses and, with a flourish, popped the cork and poured with real relief.

'"A toast to you, your news and a secure future ... bon santé..." and, as I moved closer and put my arm around her, "I love you already and I don't even know your name."

'"Françoise ... but you can call me Frankie ... everyone does."

'"Can I show you the rest of the boat?" I asked. "You will love the master suite."

'"As the Yanks say … shhhurrrr…" she slurred as I took her by the hand and led her to the cabin.

'Three days after this, Stern devoted a special forty-eight page issue of its magazine to the diaries with a print run of 2.3 million and the cover showing a picture of one black book. The headline was "Hitler Diary Discovered". *Newsweek* had made no deal with Stern but still had thirteen pages on the diaries. The *New York Times* ran front page articles for four consecutive days.

'On Monday 25th April 1983 Stern held a press conference to display the diaries for the media. It was a disaster. I thought I would be hailed as a hero; instead the reporters were very sceptical and wanted proof that they were genuine.

'So, back in the Stern offices my luck was running out. Trevor-Roper had backtracked saying that he realised that they had not used normal methods of verification due to time pressures on this scoop. Bastard. There was so much controversy that the editor was trying to establish authenticity once and for all. He had sent the diaries to the Federal Archives for a scientific report. The results of their investigations were just in. The paper of all three volumes contained a substance that had not been manufactured until 1953. The labels were all typed on the same machine. The ink came from an artist's shop. The 1943 diary was less than a year old. They were all fakes.

'The editor rang the fraud squad and asked them to arrest me. He believed that I was on board *Carina*. He told them that I had defrauded Stern of 9 million marks … The *Hitler Diaries* had not passed forensic analysis. Somehow I had been taken for a fool and wrongly accused of involvement in a scam by that scum – the forger Kajau.

You can read all about him. That is my story … I was ruined.'

'But there was so much work. I cannot believe that one man could have forged all those volumes on his own. Is it not possible that the East Germans were forging them and planting their work on the little man who just collated and bound them?' asked Alex.

'I have no idea,' replied a dejected Gerd. 'It is time for me to go. I am too distressed to eat anything. All I can say is that all the people who owned that wretched yacht were disgraced or had an early demise. Leave it alone.'

'Please let me ask what happened to *Carina*. Do you know?'

'I still owed the yard 100,000 for the refit and was in hock to the bank. I had hoped to pay off my debts when the story was published. In court I was accused of stealing 1.7 million marks; not true. I spent four years in jail and the boat was auctioned by the bankruptcy guys. I never saw her or my possessions again; good riddance.'

'Talking of possessions … did you know of any stolen art works that Goëring was said to have hidden on board?'

Gerd was angry. He replied that he knew nothing of any paintings and ranted about that devil Konrad Kujau being the only one to know about paintings; he had made a fortune after jail by selling advertised forgeries. 'But he is dead, as are the others, and I am still alive!' With that he stomped out of the room and Alex had to run to catch him and utter thanks for his trouble; hugging his frail coated skeleton and wishing him well.

As he wandered away, head bent, Gerd muttered 'I wish I had never supped with the Devil,' and looked back; tears running down his sallow cheeks. Alex waved a fond farewell.

Back in his room Alex poured himself a soft drink from the mini-bar and collapsed on the bed to think. There were so many obscure details with the Heidemann debacle; most would probably never be solved. He decided to skip lunch and enjoy a walk through the Old Town, stopping at a tavern for another bowl of their delicious goulash, before packing and preparing for a very early start in the morning. The brisk automated voice on his home phone asked him to leave a message; he did.

At the airport ticket desk Alex was able to upgrade to business class and found he was sitting next to a young clean-shaven Indian, wearing a bright white turban. His name was Darpak, which meant 'god of love'. Instead of sleeping, Alex became engaged in a long conversation about the medical problems in the United States, and how thousands of Americans were now travelling with Air India, at low cost, to have surgical procedures they were unable to afford in their own country. After what seemed like hours of non-stop details of how medical tourism had become big business in cities such as Mumbai, Alex wished for some peace to think over all he had learnt in Germany, and prepare himself for his homecoming.

Nine

All flights were on time. The first left Hamburg at seven o'clock in the morning European time, and arrived in Atlanta at midday, giving Alex only one hour to exercise away his cramp, enjoy a good coffee and find his connection to Jacksonville. He was looking forward to sleeping in his own bed, after ten days of hotel rooms, and cooking some Sunday special for Mary and Jake the next day. Unable to keep from yawning he made his way to the descending escalator thinking how glad he was to be back.

Mary had made her usual early Saturday visit to Anastasia Athletics Club for the Aqua Aerobics class, followed by twenty laps of the pool. With her friend from work, Julie, she had just joined the beginners' yoga class and looked forward to Wednesday evenings. The two of them had become close since Alex had been on his travels, and found they had much in common. Julie had recently gone through a distressing divorce from her self-employed husband, who was finding little work in the increasingly demanding world of computer maintenance. When Mary listened to her friend's complaints she often heard the mental jingle of ringing bells. As yet she had not confided her own concerns, but knew that she would; when the time was right. She found herself vaguely irritated to have to make this airport trip as she had needed to cut short her time with her mother in order to complete the weekend chores around the house.

As she waited outside the arrivals' door, she was happy that Alex was not delayed.

'Hi, hon,' she greeted him as he wheeled his small case to the trunk. 'You look weary. Don't tell me any of your news until we are home. I have been worried; you haven't exactly spent much time on the phone these past few days.'

Alex quickly detected an edge to her voice, jumped into the passenger seat and pecked her on the cheek, smelling chlorine in her hair. 'Sorry, the pay phones were hard to figure and the hotel calls would have been expensive. However, I do have a great story to tell you – when I have caught up with some sleep. I have been travelling for sixteen hours. I changed in Atlanta to save you a trip to Orlando. Thanks for meeting me.'

About to have a go at him, Mary just stopped in time. Instead she described how Jake had been working overtime on his story and was bursting to tell Alex of his findings. He was also keen to hear all the details of his father's trip. 'But not tonight,' she added as they drove towards their house. It was Alex's turn to feel put out. What right did Mary have to tell him what to do or not to do? She was becoming very bossy in her middle age.

Jake met them on the front verandah, took his father's case and carried it upstairs before joining his parents for a hot drink at the kitchen bar.

'Tell me if you heard enough from the English lady and German jailbird to be able to write something decent. Then I will go to bed. Tomorrow's a big day – we have a tennis knockout at the club.'

'The answer is definitely yes. But everything is not what it seems. Barbara, the English lady, was great fun and very generous and I quickly grew to like the German jailbird. Off you go – I will fill you in tomorrow.'

'Not before I tell you that I have found the e-mail address of the present owner – through a blog. Night.'

'And I am dragging you to bed right now,' said Mary.

Patting her on the butt Alex admitted, 'That's the second best thing I have heard tonight.'

'To sleep!' was Mary's reply.

After a restless night of tossing and turning and dreaming of skies tinted with every colour in the paint box, smoking brushwood, dead black trees and high raging orange flames, Alex rose early and shut himself away in his study to organize his papers and answer e-mails. He found a note on his desk from Jake giving him the e-mail address of someone called Sara who had been involved with *Carina*. There were no details so he sent her a message: 'Good morning. My name is Alex Johnson. I have been researching the story of the yacht *Carina* for a book. Would you be interested in meeting?'

'No. I do not want to discuss the subject,' was the curt reply half an hour later.

Not to be diverted Alex then read through the garbled Internet conversations between Sara and a German who had been interested in purchasing the yacht the previous year. He had written in some detail of the yacht's adventures but in German; the English translation was difficult to follow. He did mention, however, that an American friend of Sara's had helped to run the yacht as they cruised along the Mediterranean coast. Her name was Anita Merritt and she now resided in Baltimore. An exhaustive search for Anita's phone and/or e-mail address followed. A testy hour passed before the salty aroma of grilled bacon, wafting in from the kitchen, added to his delight at being given a number and address by the operator. It could wait until after breakfast he decided, leaning back in the swivel chair - hands behind his head to stretch.

'Cowboy breakfast today,' Jake told him as he lifted the

bean pan lid. 'I'm off to the Tennis Club soon but wanted to see you before I left.'

'If you are waiting to hear if I have made contact the answer is yes and no. I had a brush off from the owner but have found a number for her friend Anita, who I will ring after I have enjoyed this.' Alex helped himself to a plateful and sat on a stool next to his son.

'Thanks for the notes you left me – very helpful. I am beginning to feel rather like a private detective ... following clues all over the world to discover a plot...'

'Leading to ... you don't know what,' Jake finished, grinning. 'Must go, Dad. Good luck.'

It was only after Alex had cleared away the plates and made himself a coffee that he wondered where Mary had got to. He took the stairs two at a time and opened their bedroom door to find the bed neatly made but his wife was nowhere to be seen. She must have gone for a jog, he thought, so returned to his desk and rang Anita's number. After five tones his call was answered by an automaton, instructing him to leave a message and number. He added a request for her e-mail address and sat waiting impatiently; fiddling with a pen. The call was soon returned.

'Hi, this is Anita. You asked for my e-mail address. Can you tell me what you want on the phone or even on the webcam? Do you have one?' she asked in a gentle voice.

'Great,' Alex said. 'I didn't expect such a prompt reply. Yes I have a webcam but have never used it. If you give me time I will check it out and get back to you.' He told her his name and the nature of his enquiry before ringing off and looking through the instruction book. Within ten minutes they were both linked and each could see a slightly blurred and jerky version of the other.

'That was easy. What a weird way of meeting someone. You look great,' Alex said.

'And you. I was expecting a German gentleman, and you look American.'

'I am. A married writer with one grown son, and I live in Florida – does that cover things for a start?'

'As you have been upfront with me, and I believe I can trust you, I will tell you that I am an unmarried art teacher working here in Baltimore. What can I do to help?'

Alex told her about his book research and how he had hoped to meet with Sara to discuss her life on board *Carina* . . .

Anita butted in. 'Sara will not talk about those days with anyone. They were very harrowing and she still has outstanding legal matters that prohibit her from talking to strangers. I have many of the details, however, and several newspaper articles that would be useful.'

Alex looked hard at the attractive, no beautiful, image before him and rushed to suggest that maybe they could meet.

'Yes. I am working up to the Christmas break but maybe you could fly up here for a weekend if that would suit. Think about it and send me an e-mail with your decision.'

'Done,' said Alex, 'I will be in touch soon . . . thanks. I look forward to meeting the real you.'

'Same here. Talk later.'

Wow! Alex thought, as he switched off the machine, leant back in his chair and watched the birds flying around the palm trees outside his window. Did he hear them call 'What was that, what was that; told you so, told you so; ha-ha-ha?' He felt a nervous excitement that reminded him of first dates, all those years ago, and queried the significance of such emotions. His next thought was of the atmospherics that lay ahead when he put his plan to Mary.

* * *

The wind was northerly and cold, whipping against Mary's cheeks and hair and she regretted not having worn her blue and orange Florida Gators' cap. She jogged along the beach for fifty paces and then walked briskly for fifty, occasionally stopping to pick up an unbroken shell and put it in her jacket pocket. The fresh air was sweeping away the cobwebs in her brain caused by an unsettled night. Tossing and turning in time with Alex's snoring she had played and replayed her dissatisfactions. Perhaps spending so much of her life alone was number one on the list. How she longed for the companionship she had lacked as an only child with no brothers or sisters. Number two was the growing realization that she was not happy with the lacklustre attention she received from her husband when he was around. They had never had what she would term a 'loving relationship'; no gentle touching, no compliments and recently no sex. She had found her new friendship with Julie, who treated her with respect and care, more satisfying and to be honest – exciting. Mary had even begun to wonder if she was happier in the company of women than men. The last was, of course, their financial situation. She had been able to buy nice things for her home with the small gifts of money her mother had given her, but felt 'put on' every time she paid the house bills and bought the weekly grocery shop. There were plenty of things she needed and could never afford. In other words, her marriage was all take and no give.

With these issues still unresolved she crossed the road and walked along the pavement to her house; at least she had something to be proud of she reminded herself. Alex appeared as she slammed shut the screen door and removed her shoes.

'Hey, I wondered where you were. Can I get you any breakfast? I have made a pot of coffee; why don't we relax in the living room while I tell you all about my trip to Europe?'

'Fruit and yoghurt would be great, thanks; along with a large mug of coffee.'

While his wife enjoyed her breakfast Alex tried to make his travels sound interesting, but Mary showed no real interest or enthusiasm. Her mind was on other matters. He did arrest her attention, however, as he began to stutter something about further investigations.

'... and Anita has all the information I need to continue the story,' she heard him say.

'Let me get this clear,' she said, wishing she had been concentrating on his monologue. 'You have just returned from a long and expensive trip to Egypt, a two-week jaunt to England and Germany, and now you are planning to wing off to Baltimore. Is that really necessary?'

Alex was put on the defensive. 'It is my work ... what I do. Surely you can understand that ... after so many years.'

'Maybe that is the whole problem. You have been traipsing up and down the country for too many years ... with no viable results. We still can't make ends meet.'

'Believe me, it is different this time. I have a great story ... maybe a bestseller ... and I am enjoying writing again.'

'Well that's good news. When are you planning to go to Baltimore?'

'I need a couple of weeks to write up my notes, read around the subject and transcribe the tapes, so I will try to buy a return for the weekend after.'

There was a good deal of cynicism in her voice as Mary suggested that this should give them both time to sort out other serious matters before he left.

'What sort of matters?' Alex asked, and was shattered to hear her reply.

'I have been thinking of asking you for a trial separation ... it feels as if we have come to the end of the road ...

the feelings we once felt for each other have faded away.' Alex found he was shaking; whether from anger or fright he could not tell. All he could say was, 'Let's leave this discussion to later – when I have had time to think.'

Caught by Jake in the act of pouring himself a double Early Times Kentucky whisky on the rocks, before retreating to his office, he found it impossible to say anything other than 'Hi.'

Ensconced back in his swivel chair he rattled the ice round and around in the glass, took a large gulp and thought 'how apt' ... the Early Times whisky was good. Shrugging his shoulders, and clearing his throat, he switched on the Sony and started to trawl through flight schedules.

Jake knocked before entering and asked his father if he had a few minutes to talk.

'I am worried about you and Mom,' he blurted out before flinging himself down on a seat by the window. All she could talk about while you were away was how she could have her friend to stay here. It would help with the outgoings she says. It feels as if she wants to give you the heave-ho ... tell you to find your own place. But what about me? Where would I go? And why?'

'I am as much in the dark as you are,' his father told him. 'She has not mentioned anything about this before today. I really need to work things through with her and find out if I can help. Mom is obviously experiencing a "down" and I had not realized that I was part of her problem ... not paying her the attention she needs. Can we have another chat when the two of us have had more time to work this out?'

'Fine,' said Jake and hesitated before opening the door. 'I love you both but could not stay here with just two old bats forever on my case.'

'Thanks for your vote, pal,' said his father, 'you are the best.'

When Alex had booked his air ticket and finished his drink he drove to the store, returning home with several bags of groceries. Next he set about beating three large pork chops with a rolling pin between leaves of kitchen towel. He was dipping the wafer-thin snitzels in egg, herbed flour and breadcrumbs when Mary burst into the kitchen.

'What do you think you are doing, Alex?' she shouted, 'you will wreck the worktops.'

'I am making pork snitzels with noodles and red cabbage with apple for our supper. I thought you would like to try this German dish, which I enjoyed in Hamburg. Calm down…'

This increased her anger. 'It would be fine if you just told me what you were planning … then I would be prepared for all your noise and mess. In any case, I am into organic foods and vegetarian recipes. I am out tonight at the health club and will have supper there with my friends.'

'I see,' said a chastised Alex. 'That will mean more for Jake and me,' he said under his breath and returned to his supper preparations. 'Oh, by the way, just to let you know … I will be flying up to Baltimore for the weekend after next. You have plenty of time to make arrangements with your friends, but remember to provide ample food for Jake – he is looking very thin and does so much exercise.'

'And who are you to talk of caring for our son? That is something I have been doing for seventeen years with little help from you.'

Alex turned to his wife and put his hands on her shoulders.

'I don't know what has got into you Mary,' he told her. 'We have had a calm, well organized, family life with little strife … up until now. Jake is a balanced and thoughtful son who had done well at school and will be entering university in less than a year. He has many hobbies and friends; best of all he loves and respects us. You are putting all of this in jeopardy. Is that really what you want?'

Mary burst into tears and reached for the kitchen towel to wipe her face.

'Oh Alex,' she sobbed, 'I am just angry ... and confused. You are never around when I need to talk, and when you are at home you are living in another world with your books, laptop, research ... I don't know what to do.'

Alex tried to pacify her. 'My dear, our marriage is one area of my life that I felt was settled and unchanging, in a world where often mere survival is dependent on family co-operation. Let me get you a glass of wine and we can discuss this in the sitting room.'

They talked for over an hour with neither one finding comfort from the other. Both ended up more confused than before. So it was decided that they would put their problems on the back burner, until after Alex returned from Baltimore.

'My plane was delayed; I'm late for an appointment. Put your foot to the pedal,' Alex told the driver as he climbed into a taxi at Baltimore Airport.

'The cops are everywhere ... I'll do what I can. Where do you want to go?'

'The Pier 5 Hotel, Eastern Avenue; on the water,' Alex told him, peering out of the window. 'I see what you mean. What's going on?'

'There's some sort of protest march down in the docks.'

'Every city has this; so much disruption. I'm likely to miss my appointment.'

'I'll try the back route.'

'When we do arrive I will drop off my case while you

wait, and then you can take me to the old ship *Constellation* – to save time.'

'You have a meeting on that old boat?' the driver asked and was told, 'no, at the restaurant next door.'

When he eventually arrived at the restaurant Alex searched the terrace for the face he had seen on his screen. A smart slim blonde stood up and waved her paper in his direction. He walked towards Anita's table, shook her hand, then sat in the chair next to hers; overlooking the bay.

'So sorry to be late; my flight was delayed on takeoff. I thought you may have changed your mind,' he said, studying her every move and expression. 'Me too,' she replied.

She had a smooth yet animated face, with smile lines around her blue eyes and each side of her generous mouth. As she smiled her white even teeth reminded Alex of toothpaste advertisements. He guessed her age at around forty. She wore a full-length dark blue wool coat with a wraparound scarf collar and angora beret to match. 'I do hope you were not too cold sitting here. Why don't we go inside?' he suggested. As they walked into the dining room together Alex wondered why he felt so considerate to a complete stranger, deciding that she had no 'side', was very friendly and most attractive.

Anita was also sizing up her companion. He was more handsome than she had expected from their brief meetings on the webcam: fit – with a gentle face, a good head of hair, and an old-fashioned manner. She liked him.

'What an interesting harbour; full of old world character,' Alex said as he helped remove her coat and pulled out her chair. 'The food smells delicious … what do you recommend? I'm hungry.'

'The fish is delicious, but rather pricey.'

'As this is our first date the lunch is on me. We will negotiate terms for future occasions.'

She chuckled and handed him the wine menu. 'In that case what do you say to us celebrating with a glass or two of Chardonnay?'

'Well, I have just returned from a trip to Germany where I found that their Riesling grape worked well with fish. I see they have one. Would you like to try it?'

'That's fine by me. I am dying to hear why you are here, but let's enjoy lunch first and talk business later. It may be much later, for I have a very favourite place that I would like to take you to. First tell me how long you will be staying.'

She reminded herself not to rush this; the whole experience was so special. Simultaneously he was wondering about her unpredictability, and if he could possibly keep up with her. Reluctantly he confided that his flight back was at six o'clock the following evening. Not long.

Ignoring her determination a few moments ago to pace this friendship, Anita found herself replying, 'Next time it will be my turn to fly south. I always long to see the sun after a hard winter: maybe for the Easter break?'

We have only been together for twenty minutes, Alex thought, looking at his watch, and already we are planning further meetings. Wow! Go easy, old man.

The weather was fine, if cold, so after a delightful lunch they decided to walk through the city. Despite persistent questioning Alex had been unable to discover their destination and was surprised and delighted when they came to a stop outside the Baltimore Museum. They leisurely followed the arrows to the Cone Wing. A touch-screen virtual tour at the entrance answered all his queries.

In 2000 Kathy Rothkopk had become the Curator of European Painting and Sculpture at the museum and set about presenting the lives and treasures of the Cone sisters in a newly renovated wing. In 1950 the collection of Claribel and Etta Cone had been bequeathed to the citizens of Baltimore in order for them to enjoy and appreciate modern art. Now the 3,000 paintings, prints, drawings, sculpture, illustrated books, decorative arts and jewellery had a new home. The old large white galleries were transformed with dramatic colours, lighting, polished hardwood floors and new sculpture pedestals; with parts divided off to offer more intimate domestic warmth, in keeping with the works which had once adorned the walls of the sisters' Baltimore apartments. The collection of the paintings by Matisse, many painted just for Etta, was the largest in the world, and was accompanied by the works of Cezanne, Renoir, Gauguin, Manet and van Gogh.

When they had taken in the introduction Anita pulled him away with, 'Now come and see this amazing collection.'

'I had no idea that so many French masterpieces existed in America. I thought they were all in the Louvre. I suppose it is some recompense for those extraordinarily beautiful paintings by American artists in the Museum in Giverny, near Paris.'

'How did you know about those; have you been to Paris?' Anita asked delightedly.

'Unfortunately not. I have read all about Manet's influence over the *plein air* artists and how they all visited his wonderful gardens, with Chinese style bridges over lily ponds, and that an American Gallery was built nearby to show the way visiting students developed those early ideas. I would love to go there.'

'That has always been a dream of mine,' she said, slightly taken aback. 'Maybe we could go together some day?'

Alex decided to tease her. 'We will have to get to know each other before we decide such matters,' then abruptly changed the subject. 'Look over there. I have seen many prints of that figure…'

Smiling, Anita said: 'That figure is Matisse's *Large Reclining Nude*, which he painted in 1935. Do you think it could be Etta? Matisse visited the sisters here in 1930 and there is a certain likeness. He was criticized by the art world for failing to idealize the female form but she is something else, isn't she? I bring some of my senior pupils here for their art projects and they are fascinated by this lady. They say she is "with it".'

Alex walked over to look closely at *Mother and Child* by Picasso. Turning to Anita he mused '...this was so very different from the later work by Picasso. What a change in style over thirteen years. I am more conservative and prefer this painting, which is so delicate and true.'

They spent over an hour gazing at the collection before Anita suggested, as it was nearly five o'clock, they should move on.

'Would you mind coming back with me to my hotel room to discuss *Carina*?' Alex asked.

'Not at all, if you promise to be good.'

'Hey,' Alex protested, 'remember that I am an old-fashioned married man.'

They had descended the curving staircase and were back on the street before he heard her response. 'And they can be the worst.'

In Alex's rather shabby room they sat across from one another in chintzy arm chairs, with the recorder between them on a high table. They had chosen drinks from the mini-bar and found the ice machine at the end of the corridor.

'So, what do you want to know?' Anita asked, and Alex told her to start at the very beginning.

'It will take a while – if you want me to go on to the end. I have prepared a travelogue.'

'My father was given a Diplomatic appointment in Cairo in 1980 and my mother, older sister and I, joined him there and lived in some style for five years. I was a teenager and loved our International School – mainly because we only attended in the mornings and enjoyed all the water sports in the afternoons. My sister loved deep-sea diving and I followed her example by taking courses at the diving school. All the scuba instructors were men except Sara – the first female diver in Egypt. She had married an Egyptian businessman that year and they had a beautiful yacht, which we used to discover good reefs and shipwrecks. In 1985 I entered the Paris Lycée and my family moved back to the States. That same year Sara and her husband were looking for a smaller wooden family boat with some character and found just what they wanted at an auction in Hamburg: *Carina*. By June they had all the necessary electrical and engine updates that were needed to sail her to Spain and then the South of France. I heard this news from my mother and wrote to ask if I could crew on the boat for the three-month vacation. They rang to tell me that they could do with my help; so I joined them in Mallorca or Majorca, as it is often called by English speakers.

'It was my first visit to Spain and it was love at first sight. As I tried not to trip down the steps of the Air France 737 – otherwise known as 'Fat Albert' – the hot oleander-scented air, the flailing sails in the fields of windmills, the fertile red earth and the urgent calls of the cicadas won me over; and that was before I saw the clear aquamarine waters and soft white sands of Palma Bay.

'Sara met me in her bright-yellow open Mahari jeep and we speeded to the yacht club where the yacht was moored on their longest floating jetty. Her shiny white hull, and many coats of varnish, sparkled in the evening sun as I joined their group of friends for cocktails under the new, fringed awning. I sat on the deck next to the

Carina's Belgian captain and the German mechanic who had worked on the boat before joining the crew, and heard their story of the trip south from Germany. They had been beset by foul weather but the yacht had proved herself seaworthy and the three re-conditioned engines had allowed them to make good speed, even across the Bay of Biscay.

'The captain gave me a guided tour of the yacht and showed me my cabin, which was under the deck where we were sitting: approached by a small staircase also leading to the Master suite and a small office/library. The two male and one female crew (who was to join us later) had their quarters in the forepeak, beyond the galley. *Carina* was much smaller than their previous yacht and I hoped we would all be able to get on with each other in the confined space; on an extended cruise.

'I need not have worried. By day we commuted from the Marina to the island bays of Santa Ponsa, Illetas, Camp de Mar and Andraitx to the west and Cabo Blanco to the east. We lazed on deck, diving from the stern and swimming ashore to visit the local beach bars for paella or grilled fish and salad. Each evening we returned to the marina where our dockage was sternly overlooked by the unfinished cathedral on the hill. Palma was full of delights and gastronomic adventures. After a light supper on the aft deck of *Carina* our group would meander up the Avenidas – the central walkway lined on both sides by plane trees found in most Spanish cities – to lounge in the red velvet seats of the Guitar Centre, drinking strong coffee and brandy and listening to the feverish plucking of the classical guitars.

'On other evenings we would visit Edwardo's fish restaurant in the old port, the Reina del Leon for lamb shanks in garlic and tomato sauce (a recipe from central Spain) or content ourselves with a variety of snacks from

El Pilon, a tapas bar. When Sara was more inclined towards formality, we all dressed in our fineries and headed for a grand dinner at El Patio in the Plaza Gomilla followed by a show at Titos – an open-air amphitheatre. On one occasion we crammed into the Mahari and drove out of town to a smoky den called the Cassa Diablo. The old beams were decorated with every type of home-made sausage disinfected by rising smoke from fierce fires below. Of course we insisted on freshly made produce – I think the ceiling hangings were just for show.

'One evening Iraj, Sara's Egyptian husband, took us all to a bar on the top of the rising ground above El Torrente (a now dry river bed which once carried storm water runoffs from the narrow streets). We had seen little of Iraj during the past weeks and were told he was involved in hotel ventures with his Spanish partners. This particular evening he was overjoyed to have signed lucrative contracts that were newsworthy. Ricky Lash, an American newsman, ran this bar and wrote a popular gossip article in the English language *Majorca Daily Bulletin*. He combined the two by interviewing any visiting celebrities live on his local radio broadcast. That evening Iraj was, literally, the talk of town and this unusually shy man loved the attention.

'Afterwards on leaving the bar he turned left, instead of right, and hurtled the Mahari down a curving flight of eighty narrow steps to the street below. Thus he started the famous 'Steps Club'. Any driver brave enough to ascend or descend these steps in their vehicles was given a special membership tie by Ricky Lash. Many years later I returned to find three posts had been set in concrete to bar the way.

'That summer we also cruised around the Balearic Islands. First we visited Menorca to the north east of Mallorca, which had a wonderful history as Nelson's Mediterranean base. The island was flat with narrow waterways cutting into the land rather like fiords. We stayed a few days in Mahon harbour – fishing, swimming, drinking Soborano brandy and eating plenty of locally grown olives and almonds – before heading back to Pollensa Bay on the north-east tip of Mallorca. Here we stocked up the ice box and larder for a few days moored off the deserted military island of Cabrera with its blissful peace by day and phosphorescent sea by night. We snorkelled into caves; swimming amongst darting swathes of multi-coloured fish. An American sailboat arrived on our third day and we were asked to join them for Salty Dogs. All I can remember about that day is the terrible thirst I had after drinking from a salty-rimmed glass; and the resultant headache.

'We continued south for Ibiza and the plan was to spend a month exploring this unusual island. After a five hour crossing we sailed into Ibiza harbour and anchored off the lighthouse; reversing back to tie our stern to the bollards on the promenade. We were alongside a fishing boat and they displayed their catch – for us to choose our supper. It would take a month of Sundays to describe the pleasures of that island. The town of Ibiza was buzzing with the Jet Set. The narrow streets bulged with hippy-style clothes, glittering bags, jewellery and local arts and crafts. The tiny shops with street displays were interspersed with bars and bistros, cafés and restaurants – all teaming with excitable holidaymakers. The nightlife was positively exotic as the wonderful warm night-time climate encouraged garden discos, cabarets and film shows. The food of Ibiza was delicious: oven-baked Spanish loaves laced with Moroccan sauces and spices; fresh crisp salads and juicy home-grown fruits; freshly baked bread and enseimadas. The beaches of San Antonio must have been world beating with young, topless beauties everywhere and bronzed naked men zipping over the waves on surf boards. Those who took a short walk from the sea and up the hill were rewarded. Whole fish, a foot long, were baked in salt in the classic kitchens of the old town and the flans were to die for.

'Half an hour's sail away was the sand-banked island of Formentera, with the pink coral fringe on the water's edge dividing sea from golden dunes, anchored by clumps of reeds. Back from the beach was a bamboo shelter with benches, tables and a charcoal barbecue which glowed by midday ready for shrimp and squib kebabs and the occasional lobster tail, carried on trays on our heads as we waded from *Carina*. Our enormous cool box was full of beer, wine and coke. We wore very little - sun hats, sun glasses and sun cream.'

'No clothes?' Alex asked in amazement. 'Well the shy wore G-strings,' she replied, pretending to look coy.

'You will understand how sad I was when the month was over and we spent our last few days in Spain re-stocking with food and fuel for the long trip to southern France, where a mooring had been booked for *Carina*. I had to return to America with a heavy heart bound by a cordon bleu cookery course I had arranged for the winter. I was to return to *Carina*, however, the following summer.'

'This seems a good moment to pause for a break from the past,' Alex suggested, 'and to talk of the present. I would like to know more about what you do here in Baltimore. It must seem very tame after your adventures in Europe.'

'Oh no, those hedonistic days are long gone. The experiences I had in my twenties will last me a lifetime. When my father retired, my parents bought a bungalow here on the water and after taking a teaching course I found a job to be near them. I was engaged to be married to a soldier once. Six months before our planned wedding he lost his life at the start of 'Desert Storm' – the first Iraq War in response to Saddam invading Kuwait. My father died a year later and I moved in to keep my mother company. I have been with her ever since – seventeen years.'

'What a time you have had. It makes my blinkered life seem so very ordinary – I have been living "in the box" as they say. Recently I have been wondering if it could be time to jump out.'

'Talking of boxes, my mother and I want to ask you a question: would you come home with me to meet her? I have told her about your project and she would like you to join us for supper in our boxlike apartment.'

Alex stood and reached for their coats. 'Lead the way,' he instructed, 'I would love to. But does this mean that I will have you to myself tomorrow morning to finish your story?'

'I can meet you at ten after Church, if that suits you.'

Better not push my luck, Alex thought to himself as he agreed; but he didn't want to waste a minute. He had to steel himself not to hold her hand as they walked along the street, or take her in his arms in the lift to their apartment. He had an urgent desire to kiss the back of her neck as she put her key in the door. He could smell, almost taste, her lily of the valley perfume and was lost in a craving to know everything there was to know about this woman.

Her mother was charming; greeting him as a friend. She filled in a few of the gaps by finding albums of her daughter's adventures, which included postcards and letters from all the places of interest Anita had visited. The evening passed quickly as they chatted about world events and laughed about the many tricky moments they had all experienced. It was too soon over. Alex kissed them both on the cheek and made a hasty exit, saying he would meet Anita at his hotel around ten. He asked them both to join him for lunch at the nearby 'Seafood Factory' after he and Anita had wrapped up their recording session.

'Can you imagine how wonderful it was to be living on *Carina* for the summer of 1986 ... in the South of France?' Anita asked, as they settled down to their task.

'No ... please tell me,' Alex replied, wishing that she could sit there next to him telling her tale forever. Once again he stayed cool and turned on the recorder.

'There have been so many Hollywood films which show the mountainous backdrop ... dissected by narrow roads with hairpin bends leading to deep blue bays; surrounded by pine trees and Edwardian mansions. It was all true. I flew into Nice at the end of June and found the yacht in the marina, as planned. Jill, the new crew, made me feel very welcome, telling me that everyone was on the beach, and suggesting that I had a rest before they returned. Instead I quickly unpacked my rucksack and changed into a bikini and cotton shift and, collecting a towel from the linen cupboard, walked over to the beach.

'The water was still very cold, but the sun was hot and I still had enough time to start work on my tan. I fell asleep the instant I lay on the towel and the cooling breeze woke me several hours later; luckily I had used plenty of sun cream. Sara and Iraj seemed very pleased to see me when I boarded the boat to find them sitting on the deck with a tall glass jug of Pimm's. As I sipped from my fruit-filled glass they described the itinerary planned for the next two months – starting that evening as they had tickets for the Nice Concert Hall to hear the singer Jessye Norman, and I was included in the party. They asked me to be responsible for all the catering on board and Sara said she would show me the best superstores and markets to visit. Of course, she added, they would often be eating ashore and on those evenings I would only have to look after the crew.'

Alex stopped her at this point. He wanted to know whether she was treated as a servant or a family member.

'That is the fantastic part of this whole story ... I always felt like a friend or sister to Sara and a daughter to Iraj, who was much older. I loved catering for them and they enjoyed my company on the many outings we had together. The other three were more like proper crew – working to keep the yacht clean and running well – but I suppose I was rather like an au pair. Later, when everything went wrong, it was the close-knit nature of this arrangement that saved us all from going mad.'

'Was the south of France as exciting as Spain had been?'

'... a difficult question to answer; the two countries were so different. In France the sea was not as warm or clean and we saw very few fish; there were no uninhabited islands and the beaches were short on sand and long on crowds. The French cuisine however was more sophisticated and artistic, and their markets were bursting to the seams with freshly picked reasonably priced produce. French cities like Nice or Cannes were more up-to-date with large department stores stocking designer clothes and furniture. Visitors had all the arts to choose from: galleries, classical concerts, ballet, street operas and big-top circus competitions. In addition to all the water sports there were events such as world tennis and golf tournaments, car races and rallies, swimming galas and horse racing. Never a dull moment.'

'And did you spend most of the time in the marina or did you cruise?'

'We sailed along the coast to Menton, on the border between Italy and Monaco, for cheaper fuel and to listen to James Galway in concert in the square of the Basilica of St Michael. We spent several nights in the Monaco Marina and dined by candlelight in the Hotel Miramar, visiting the much-filmed casino afterwards. Once we visited their tiered night club. Every Friday, after the cabaret, the roof slid open for an overhead fireworks display. Iraj enjoyed golf and we spent several days in the huge marina at Antibes so he could meet his golfing buddies at the Mandelieu or Mougins courses. I suppose you could say our cruising was in order to be in the right place at the right time for the many attractions.'

'Did you visit St Tropez to see Brigitte?' Alex asked, half joking. 'I read somewhere that she was a pet fanatic and ran a shelter for homeless dogs and cats. Is that correct? It seems a far cry for her glamorous film persona.'

'Indeed we did, although there was no sign of Brigitte. In the bay of St Tropez the yachts arrived in swarms from four o'clock onwards and backed onto the town promenade. This was an apt word for each evening the townsfolk promenaded up and down, staring into each yacht in turn. Their enjoyment was curtailed when, for fun, the crews of all the central yachts placed enormous vases of gladioli on their aft decks; behind which their owners could sit in full evening dress, sipping Champagne and playing cards without feeling like monkeys in a cage.

'The small town was crowded every evening with smart visitors jostling for gifts in the boutiques and pushing to secure the best harbourside tables at the cafés. Meanwhile, in the tree -lined park behind, children played with hoops or skipping ropes, their mothers sat on benches busy with their crochet hooks, and elderly gentlemen threw boules. Their simple lives differed little from those of past generations.'

Alex was fascinated by this full account, with no 'ums', 'you knows', 'urrs' or long pauses and was very grateful that she had taken time to write her story. This would make transcribing his tapes so much easier. Was there no end to the abilities of this interesting lady?

The 'lady' wondered what reaction he would have to her next suggestion. She didn't want to interfere in any way with his proposed book, but thought he might enjoy Sara's own story of the *Carina* disaster as well as her own.

Ten

Anita sat back in her chair and mentally scanned the ominous events of that autumn. She had always planned to leave France and return to the United States at the end of the summer, knowing that the yacht was due to be laid up in the Antibes Marina for the winter; Iraj had projects to oversee in other countries and had bought the yacht for the summer months. So when he returned one afternoon, after a golf game, to tell them that his plans had changed, she was as taken aback as Sara and the skipper.

'I have just heard that the planning permission to build my new hotel in Hurghada stipulates that it must be completed in three years,' he told us as we gathered in the saloon. 'This means that I must sail *Carina* to Egypt; so I have to ask you all if you will stay on as crew until we reach my home port.' Skip, Hans the engineer and Jill (who was now his girlfriend) all agreed. They had no other jobs to go to and had been hoping to be able to stay on *Carina* for the winter. I told the boss that I would have to check with my parents, but loved the idea.

'Ring them right now,' Iraj instructed, 'then we can make plans.'

My father answered the call and told me that it was all right with him and passed me on to mother. She sounded worried; telling me that Egypt was a dangerous place and to take special care.

'I hope you are not involved with any foreign men,' she said, and had to be reassured.

So it was decided. I would be taking the longest sea journey of my life.

The six of us sat around the saloon table with notebooks, and a large chart of the Mediterranean, planning this epic voyage in minute detail. Nothing involving stores, safety, maintenance or creature comforts was forgotten.

'It is unfortunate that we need to travel in the winter,' Iraj said. 'If we port hop and hug the coast we should be safe if the weather turns foul. We have four months to have the hull cleaned, to service the engines and check the electrical systems; I need to stay here for business until the end of January.'

'How long will this journey take?' Sara asked.

The skipper replied that with a good deal of luck they should reach Egypt by early March; this was dependent on how many port calls they made and for how long.

'If we have no equipment problems and our stores are sufficient,' Sara said, looking across the table at me, 'we shouldn't need to make too many stops. What average speeds can we expect from our trials?' she asked the skipper.

'I worked out that we travelled economically on other long voyages at ten knots on the main engine, and fourteen knots if we also used the two wing engines; but that would consume eighteen to twenty gallons of diesel an hour. On our trip south from Hamburg we used up our two tanks of fuel – 250 gallons capacity each – over 400 miles of running and we used the three engines for most of the trip.'

'In that case we had better divide the journey into manageable distances of not more than three to four hundred miles or forty hours of running.'

'And how far do we have to travel?' Sara asked him, a shocked expression on her face.

'By my rough estimate it will be something like 2,000 miles,' her husband told her, 'but Skip will work it out exactly.'

Sara wrote a few figures on her pad and seemed more assured. 'That sounds like only ten days of continuous running to me, if all goes well.'

'What I was going to suggest,' said Anita, returning to the present, 'was that you read this article describing an interview given by Sara for her local paper: the *Pittsburgh Tribune-Review*. We can talk about it later. I have to go home for lunch with a neighbour of Mom's who keeps an eye on her when I am ever away. I could be back by two and we will have the rest of the afternoon together as I plan to take you to the airport.'

She handed him the paper. Alex was very disappointed. He had made all sorts of plans for the rest of the day together, and wondered if this was a sign that Anita did not like him. Little did he know that she felt so good when they were together that she had decided not to rush into this relationship. Her hope was that they would soon spend more time together; long enough to sort out their feelings.

Despite an empty ache in his chest he decided to skip lunch and settled down to read the press interview with Sara, jotting down questions to ask Anita when she returned. Skipping the long introduction he came to the part about their trip to Egypt on *Carina*.

'By the first week in February, we had left Italy, and we got into a storm. It was a horrible storm, and we were three days at sea. We slipped past the island of Crete, kind of like a ski going downhill. We couldn't turn against the waves and we ended up low on fuel. So we calculated our fuel load and figured out we wouldn't make the

Egyptian border, so we figured we'd be better off landing in a major city. So we went to Benghazi.

Benghazi, the capital of Libya, was a volatile place in 1987. The year before the United States launched a series of bombing attacks on the country in a counter-terrorism initiative. It was a few months before the end of a brutal, five-year war with neighbouring Chad.

But when the yacht needed help from the Libyan army irregulars who patrolled the coast they had no problem with us coming in. Libyan soldiers kept us in the Benghazi harbour for five days of interrogation under armed guard. I slowly began to realize that to the Libyan government we represented international media attention, untold amounts of ransom money and other potential foreign favours. We had five people from four different countries so it was like a treasure chest.

On 14th February we were taken off the boat and brought into Benghazi, to a large hotel. There we ran into a westerner who heard our story and agreed, in spite of the risk, to leave the country and try to get help. He was the main one who took the message to the West that we were there. We have never released his name. We were held in the hotel for three weeks, then taken westward to Derna, a coastal town about 150 miles away, to another hotel. The captors laid claim to three of the longest months of our lives.

We spent most of those months in the small Derna hotel waiting, conversing and smoking. I stared out the window at people passing in the street for hours upon hours. After smoking pack after pack of cigarettes we made playing cards out of the packets, drawing the suits with red and black pens. To play checkers we used silver and gold coins and drew a board on an old placemat. I still had my ship's cat with me for comfort, and tried – in spite of sharing my cramped space with the others – to get a little exercise every day, using the windowsill as a ballet barre for leg stretches. We didn't eat much, but since we hardly moved, we didn't need to. Every night we were locked in by soldiers, who told us that if we tried to leave without an escort we would be shot. They never lied to us. They said they would shoot us or release us, depending on what they were told. It was never anything personal.

Back home my parents were trying – and failing – to navigate the maze of bureaucratic protocol that could bring me home. In May, after three months of work by diplomats and the hostages' loved ones, we were released into the custody of the Belgian Consulate and sent our separate ways – except my husband, who was taken away and sent into a brutally restrictive solitary confinement; it seems my husband's family had not completed the necessary formalities. He was given a mattress on the floor in a room with no windows and taken to the toilet once a day. Those months were very hard for me too, as I waited for him to be released. Everything was on hold.

I travelled between the United States and Egypt, trying to free my husband, stay employed and keep things in order. Finally, in November, he was released. He was so shell-shocked that he stayed put and didn't make arrangements to come home until a month later. Finally we were reunited on Crete and sailed our boat back to Egypt. He had lost a lot of weight and his hair was all over the place. I read something that Terry Anderson (the Lebanese civil war hostage) wrote saying that you come up in stages, and that's really it. That's how you recover from anything emotional. Slowly, he began to try to get our old life running again. At first, all I could do was think about Libya; and after some time I realized that five minutes had passed without thinking about Libya, and then later you realize that you have spent half a day without thinking about it. It goes like that.

Back in Egypt we found that our business had gone to seed in the hands of relatives; our investment construction project, a hotel on the Red Sea, was stalled and haemorrhaging money. Family relations began to deteriorate, along with my husband's health. By 1992 he had developed stomach cancer.

I believe that if we hadn't lingered in Egypt for six months dealing with family, land and money squabbles before flying to the United States to seek treatment at Allegheny General Hospital in Pittsburgh, my husband might have been saved. In the States they all said the same thing. If you'd have come sooner, the outcome would have been different. He died in August 1993, and was buried in Homewood Cemetery in Pittsburgh.

After his death I returned to Egypt and through friends met an American from Minnesota who had spent thirty-four years in Egypt and ran an industrial storage company there. We were married in 1998 and now live back in the States.'

Alex had read extracts from the ship's log book which gave details of the storm they had encountered. As Sara had given no details for the article he was interested to have Anita's take on the voyage. He was happy that she arrived on time that afternoon, and started their discussions with this important part of the *Carina* saga.

'Can you remember how things went wrong on the day of the storm?' he asked.

'Yes, vividly. We had a happy and speedy trip south east from Menton. The weather was great. The sea was calm and we were able to spend time sunbathing on deck. We passed Corsica on the starboard side and Elba to port and stayed close to the Italian coast as far as Naples; where we moored for two days. The wind picked up as we continued through the Tyrrhenian Sea, making for Sicily, and was increasing as we safely negotiated the Straits of Messina between Sicily and the toe of Italy. Skip handed Iraj a weather report as we shot through this disturbed waterway: warning him that the winds could rise to gale force the following day.

'"Baton down the hatches," Iraj ordered, "and make full speed for Crete."

'We had 300 miles of open sea ahead of us before sighting Crete, and both Skip and Sara asked him if it would be best to shelter in some port until the storm had blown through. He chuckled and told them that it was in the hands of the gods. The following morning the winds rose from force six in the morning to force nine in the afternoon. The boat was rising above the waves and then pounding down into deep troughs. We spent most of the day huddled in the wheelhouse with blue water and strong spray pounding onto the decks and over the windows. The rotating wiper failed at midday and visibility was very poor. The autopilot was not able to work with the strong northerly following wind. Iraj called Skip away from the chart table to help him steer but even the two of them were unable to hold the course. Iraj shouted for Sara to help Skip on the wheel so that he could work out how far we were from land and use the radio, if necessary.

'It looked as if we were being driven, against our will, towards Libya. At that moment a huge wave broke completely over the boat, which shook, creaked and wallowed but recovered. Sara took one hand off the wheel and put her hand to her mouth.

'"I am going to be sick," she cried and rushed to the side door and slid it partly open only to be bowled over by a deluge of water. She fell on the floor, fainted and was washing from side to side in a foot of seawater. I grabbed her and tried to help her onto the seat, but she lost her balance again as the boat rocked from side to side, rising dolphin-like and crashing down again.

'"It's getting worse. I'll radio for help," Iraj shouted above the storm noise, "we are only fifty miles from land."

'He picked up the ship-to-shore radio and called: "This is Motor Yacht *Carina* ... encountering extreme weather ... making for Bengazi ... request permission to enter Libyan territorial waters. Radio open for response, Over..."

'Their response was instant. "Motor Yacht *Carina* ... we have you on radar. Set course for 175 degrees and notify us when you are in range of the lighthouse. We will escort you into the harbour. Over."

'"Understood. Heading for lighthouse. Please keep in radio contact. Out," Iraj responded.

'Iraj left the chart table and lifted his wife onto the Captain's seat and helped with the steering while I tried to clean her with a towel.

'"I think it is calming down a little," Skip told us. "We should sight land within a few hours. We will all feel better when I can go below to get us a hot drink." Sara groaned.

'Four hours later we sighted the sweeping search of the lighthouse and a fast customs cutter making straight for us. This was fortunate as we were very low on fuel having battled the storm for so many hours. The seas were calmer, although still rough, and Iraj had to tie himself to the railing as he awaited the approaching boat. As it came alongside they threw him a warp. Skip slid open the wheelhouse door and shouted to Iraj but his words were lost in the wind. Iraj caught the rope and tied it to the deck cleats as the uniformed captain of the cutter shouted in broken English, "We will tow you into port."

'"We do not need a tow," Iraj shouted back, but was ignored. When he returned to the wheelhouse Skip told him that he should not have taken their rope "They can claim salvage now. I tried to warn you but you could not hear me."

'We tied up against the harbour wall and tried to tidy up before eating a sandwich and falling into our bunks. The next day two army jeeps arrived and soldiers carried food and tools on board. Naturally, we thought the people welcomed us. But a customs officer arrived with papers for Iraj to sign.

'"We are very grateful for your help last night," he told them. "What are these papers?"

'The officer gave no response but asked to see our passports. Iraj pointed to his permit saying that he was allowed to travel in Libya. He added that he could not sign the papers until he was told what they meant.

'"Sign now or I arrest you," he was told, and Sara burst into tears and started sobbing.

'Through her tears she quietly told him that she would like to ring her family to tell them that she was safe, but his men had taken her phone. Could she please have it back?

'"When your husband has done what I tell him," he replied.

'Sara rushed up to him: changing her pleading to threats. She would have to talk to Gaddafi. They were important people. He pocketed our passports and took the papers from the table and beckoned to the soldiers to take Iraj away. He turned to Sara and told her to calm herself or she would be thrown in jail.

'Skip took Sara to one side and asked her to do what the officer said, or else we would all be in serious trouble. He told her these men were from the Revolutionary Guard of Libya; no one crosses them.'

Anita was silent for a few moments before adding 'and you know the rest.'

'What a terrifying experience you had: it seems etched on your memory. Unlike you, it is possible that Sara has blocked out most of the traumatic details, and doesn't want to try to recall those years; quite understandable. Can you give me more details of your time in custody?'

'I will try. When we arrived at the decrepit hotel in Derna, and were left in our locked dreary room, Skip warned us to be very careful. He had recently heard tales of boat crews being taken away and their families never seeing them again. We were terrified and talked of the possibility of bribing the guards with money or jewellery to let us make an outside call. I had hidden some dollars in my shoes. Sara needed to find out what they had done with her husband and was anxious to get some reaction from the guards. This never happened. For the three months of captivity we were moved around from one seedy place to another and were never given any news from the outside world. Sara was at her wits' end.'

'I suppose that is just about all you can tell me.'

'There are small details such as the bowls of slimy rice that were delivered on metal trays; the constant questions which the guards would not or could not answer; the mood changes we all went through – hopeful one minute and desperate another; the good feelings of comradeship often shattered by selfish rants. How prisoners cope in isolation I cannot imagine. When they survive to tell all, they often find that their life in prison had been so deprived of stimuli that there was nothing to describe but the minutae of existing from minute to minute, hour by hour, and the hell that can be created by the lonely imagination. Of course, the most poignant moment for us was the announcement by the guard that we could go home – that day. We all cheered and hugged each other. But there was the necessary question from Sara … "will my husband be joining us?" and the blank stubborn face we had become used to. "I know nothing. You will see," he told us.

'So what of *Carina*? Did they impound her?'

'As far as I know they did. There were customs disputes and legal ramifications but these must have been settled as Sara and Iraj sailed her away to Egypt the following year. I know little of what followed as I returned to the States and my family via Switzerland. Sara and I have had little contact since that time, but I have followed her trials and tribulations in the papers and on the web. I believe that the yacht was moved to a pontoon in the new marina in El Gouna, when it opened; but this was so expensive and she ended up moored to a buoy.'

'I know. I didn't tell you before ... I have been on board her there.'

'You are a dark horse! Was she in a terrible mess? She has been there for years. There has been a long struggle with the Egyptian bureaucracy over family ownership which is now over.'

Alex told her a little of what he discovered on board but time was running out. He stood, stretched, went over to Anita and lifted her up by the elbows. Slowly he kissed her forehead, both cheeks and then her mouth. They smiled at each other and Alex at last was able to haltingly, and in a breaking voice, confide his feelings.

'From the time you stood and waved at the restaurant ... well no, before, when I first saw you on the screen ... I have wanted to make love to you ... why should we wait? Having heard you describe your adventures I consider that I have always known you. What do you say?'

Anita hesitated a moment. 'Oh Alex, this is special. I would like the friendship to last forever; but I have no desire to rush into an affair with a married man, as charming as he appears to be.'

So they decided to put things on hold. As Anita drove

him to the airport Alex told her that his marriage was going through a bad patch, with his wife suggesting a trial separation. Since he had met Anita he was seeing the future through pink lenses and needed to meet her rosy self again, as soon as possible. Was that the way she felt about him? With an affirmative answer he was able to board the plane back to St Augustine with more hopeful thoughts than when he left. Things were definitely looking up.

Sitting in a window seat, his legs stretched under the chair in front, Alex shut his eyes and pretended to sleep. His daydreams were vivid and ingenious. He concocted a world where he and his vital lady Anita were eventually able to share many wild adventures - much like those of the five *Carina* owners.

Eleven

No one was waiting at the Jacksonville airport for Alex this time. At nine o'clock it was too late to find any transport other than a taxi, so he jumped into the one at the head of a queue. The costs of his travels were mounting. He knew that his book was a last throw of the dice. It was now or never he reminded himself; at the same time denying any haunting comparison with Gerd.

The house seemed empty as he unlocked the front door but Jake came rushing down the stairs to greet him.

'How did it go Dad?' he asked. 'Glad you are back ... things have not been good with Mom.'

'Hey Jake, let me settle in with a beer and we will talk...'

They sat on the verandah with their drinks as Jake told about the weekend's comings and goings.

Then Jake told him that Mary had been having another heart to heart with him. Not easy.

'Just like her to talk to you while I was away; before we had discussed our problems between ourselves and worked things out.' Alex said, staring into the dark distance.

'I know. But she says she has had enough of your lifestyle – and you are away too darned much, Dad –and she would like to "move on" whatever that means.'

'I'm not very sure ... you will have to wait until I have asked her. I have had time to think about our family while I was on the flights. I have been very switched off for the last few years ... it must have something to do with the loss of Gramps, Nan and my sister. They were all so special … and Mom has never wanted to try to fill the space left by their loss. At the same time I have not been too attentive to either of your interests. It is time to try to turn over a new leaf. Bear with me…'

'Of course. But remember that I do not want to stay with Mom and her friend if you are not here. Wasn't it your parents' house anyway?'

'Yes, but over the years Mom has converted an ordinary place into a very comfortable home. Has she been talking about her friend moving in again?'

'Well, you know … they seem to be together a lot.'

'…and have you met her?'

'Yes, and I'm not at all keen. She is very offhand; doesn't have much to say to me.'

Alex briefly searched his son's anxious face before attempting to comfort him. Jake must not worry; things would work out, he told him; yet a little voice inside his head was questioning the veracity of his reassurances.

They both went their own way; Jake thinking that his life was in turmoil, and Alex wondering about how to deal with the situation. Mary was still out with her friends, not returning until after midnight.

The following evening Alex and Mary walked to the 'A1A' pub on the Matansas River. They had both felt that it would be best to talk away from the house. They used the excuse that it was best not to involve Jake, knowing that was not possible. Jake was totally involved, but at least he did not have to hear their acrimonious discussions. Everything started reasonably well, but Alex was merely trying, unsuccessfully, to smooth things over.

'This place is a mini version of the Braukeller in Hamburg where I first met Gerd Heidemann,' he told her. 'It seems a long time ago, but it is only weeks. A great deal has happened...'

Mary looked down into her glass, her hair partially concealing her strained expression.

'Alex, this is difficult, but I have spent many lonely hours thinking it over. Our marriage has run its course. There's no spark anymore. You would be better off running after your dreams without a family round your neck.'

Alex was shaken by this direct approach. He had been hoping they could at least make attempts to patch up any disagreements. He looked over towards the next table in embarrassment as he noticed them tuning in to what Mary was saying.

'What do you want me to do ... and what about Jake? Finish your beer and we will take a walk. It is a lovely evening and there are too many ears flapping around here.'

They left the pub and walked across to the marina. As they trailed along the main jetty Alex wondered aloud how long they would be finishing the new Bridge of Lions. It had been such an upheaval for so long. Mary twisted his words; as she had done many times, Alex recalled in bewilderment.

'Like our life together!' she said.

'I had no idea that you have been so unhappy. Why didn't you say something before?'

'My God, I tried. You always had your head in the clouds. I think it was finding that yacht *Carina* that clarified matters for me. I realized that you would be so much happier living the bachelor's life on a boat, than with me.'

As they slowly walked along the river bank Alex wondered where she had got this idea. It was an idea that had never entered his head. As much as he loved boating he saw it as a hobby; purely for holidays and high days. He loved the comfort and privacy of their home. It was doubtful whether he would ever be able to replace his family life with something as satisfying.

'Jake tells me that you would like me to move out. Is that true?' he asked her.

'We could try living apart for a year … to see how things work out.'

'… and you are planning to have your friend as a live-in to help pay the bills?'

'That may work.' Mary told him abruptly.

'I certainly cannot afford to cover the house *and* my own digs … until I have published the *Carina* story. And what about Jake? Where will he live?'

'He has just over a year left at High School and he will be off to College … unless he decides to enrol here at Flagler … he hasn't even made up his mind what he really wants to study. Luckily, we saved for his fees over the past ten years. I see no problem – he can stay where he is for now.'

Alex did not hear what he was waiting for; some token of her love for her son or understanding of the predicament he would be in if his parents lived apart. It was always more difficult for an only child who had been one part of the golden number three. Instead of staying calm he found he was becoming irritated and … well, to be honest … gripped by a quiet contained fury.

'You seem to have it all worked out. There is not much else to discuss just now. You'd better get on with it,' he told her in a bitter voice. Alex turned and walked away from her. He was not seeing straight; over and over the same thought came to him, 'This is not the woman I have known and loved for so many years. She has changed, but then, so have I.' His concerns were no longer dwelling on Mary but with another lady – miles distant.

During the following week Alex concentrated on his

book. He wrote an eight page synopsis and character sketches of all those involved in the history of *Carina*. Next he collated all his references, hand writing them on the old card system he had always used; making up his mind to use his computer filing system for the next book. He was amazed to find, on reading what he had already written at the gentle rate of a few pages each day, that he was almost half way along his critical path. Pacing up and down his study (much like Goëring was known to have done) he rang Jan, his New York agent. As he anxiously ran his fingers along the desk, and packed book shelves above, he told her how very important this project was; and a few of the reasons why.

'...so you can see how very necessary it is to get this book off the ground within the next few months. Have you got the time to help me?'

Her answer was sweet to his ears: 'Send me the title, synopsis and first five chapters as attachments to your e-mail and I will get back to you with my suggestions. How does that suit?'

Jan was the most efficient person he had ever met and he was happy to have her in control. He needed all the help he could find as the rest of his life was falling apart.

He attacked the keyboard with renewed energy and the chapters were rolling off his laserjet printer when he had the most important e-mail he had ever received. Jan had written that she loved the story and could see the way it was going. She could partly fund his work up front, if that would help, and would be happy to work on the first part of the book leaving the second half until he had finished.

'Would you like to spend the weekend at my home on Amelia Island in two weeks' time?' she wrote. 'There is a most exciting car rally on the island that Saturday. We can talk over your book and you can have a break ... invite Anita to join us if you feel like it.'

Great, she had been listening to his hints, Alex thought, and sent his thanks by return. His next e-mail was to Anita:

'Hi, sweet Anita. We have both been invited to stay with Jan my literary agent, the weekend after next. You will both get along fine. She is working on my first draft and we will have ideas and changes to discuss. I believe you and I also have things to talk about. The destination is a secret. I will arrange flight tickets – you can pick them up at the desk – and e-mail me the times later. Please confirm. Love Alex. P.S. Have you noticed that both our names start with A? Could this mean good luck?'

Alex swivelled his chair to watch a woodpecker chipping away in the maple tree outside his window, and wondered at the purity and pride of the blue-flag iris as he pictured smiling eyes of a similar hue. He was just asking himself if he was in love, and what being 'in love' could possibly mean, when his reveries were interrupted by a whistling son.

'Hi,' Alex greeted him, 'what do you have to be so happy about?'

'I won my tennis match, and the other guy was two years older.'

'Great! I must come down to the courts and watch one evening.'

'Wish you would ... but I came to ask what you and Mom have decided. It has been worrying me.'

'Oh ... hey, sit down a while ... I will fetch us a Pepsi,' Alex said as he hastily left the office to think.

Jake looked surreptitiously at his watch as his father returned and handed over a cold can.

'I haven't got long ... there's a match I want to watch ...' he told his Dad. He also was having difficulty approaching the subject they needed to explore together.

Alex cleared his throat, took a long drink of his cola,

and turned to face Jake, who flicked back his hair and found plenty of stray threads on the knees of his jeans to study. Standing like a gangly faun who can hardly bear his weight on his spindly legs, he suddenly wandered over to the desk and switched off the winking lights of the computer. Turning he asked his father – 'Well?'

'OK. It seems that you were right,' Alex told him. 'Your mother and I could be living apart for a while ... to see how it works.'

'What do you mean, how it works?' Jake asked, finding an instant temper. 'I know it won't work ... we will not be a family anymore ... just three wandering spirits doing our own thing. That is what the poor people of the Nile were doing when I was there. We are meant to be sensitive, educated folk ... families are designed to be a comfort in troubled times ... that sort of thing. Where the hell do I live?'

Alex stretched and covered his son's hand with his own. 'Whoa, cool down. We would both like you to live here at home, until you finish High School. It is only for a year and then you will be off. Listen, I have a proposition to put to you.'

'Yea...' Jake was apprehensive.

'How about working for me during the summer vacation?'

'Not writing? I can't yet reach your high standards. Besides I have my dog walking business to run.'

'No, not writing this time, but still involving Egypt. If we can stand the heat I am thinking of having *Carina* pulled out of the water for a full survey, her hull cleaned and any necessary work done to make her habitable and in full running order. Those Mercedes engines have not been turned over for years. Even your dog-owning clients know that you must have a break. Think about it.'

'Wow. It's a heck of a long way for us to travel twice in one year. And the cost...'

'Let me worry about that. I have been waiting to tell you … the idea for my book has been accepted and I should have it finished long before the summer.'

Jake came over to give his father a hug and grinned at him before joking that, maybe, the trouble he was having with Mary had got him off his butt at last. 'Way to go Dad,' he added to smooth things over.

'Don't let's count our chickens … but I should know for sure in a few weeks.'

Jake was about to leave but turned to say, 'One thought – why don't you make enquiries about bringing *Carina* over here. It would probably be cheaper to have any restoration done in our yards … and then…' he was warming to the idea, 'we could have her here in the marina. I could stay with you whenever…'

Of course that idea had been floating around in Alex's dreams for quite a time; but he attempted to look surprised and delighted with Jake's suggestion.

'That would be great, but I must find out if it is viable. She may well have been sold over there.'

Seeing Jake's face drop with disappointment he added, 'I think I will pack up now and come to watch the match with you.'

'Cool, I will go and fetch us some beer and snacks,' Jake told him, showing some renewed enthusiasm.

For the first time for many years Alex cleaned out, washed and polished his old green Ford Taurus; spraying the seats with lavender to eliminate any take-away odours and the tyres with 'Eagle 1' ultra-black glossy shine. The idea of parking his vehicle anywhere near the wide variety of classic cars presented at the Amelia Island Concours d'Elegance made him nervous, and he hoped to arrive early enough to park near – but not too near. Wary of any derogatory comments from Mary he had waited until she had been picked up by her friend, on an expedition to the Outlet Shopping Mall, before starting work on his car. He had looked at the list of cars to be judged and reckoned to spend some time looking at the classic Mercedes exhibits. There was to be a silent auction after the rally – if only. He wondered what car Anita would like him to buy 'when the boat comes in', and then laughed at his own joke.

The spruced-up Taurus looked good as it sat waiting outside the arrival doors at Jacksonville Airport; Alex had never felt better. At last he had something special to look forward to in his life. At that moment the doors rotated to reveal the trim blonde that he had spent weeks dreaming about in assorted locations. Anita waved and ran to the car, threw her bag on the back seat, and jumped in next to him.

'We were early – just as well with you parked in this loading zone,' were her first jokey words.

'I took a chance, not wanting to miss a minute, and was lucky. But first things first…' and he leant over to give her a long lingering kiss. She wore no lipstick but her lips were moist and juicy and could have been licked forever but, appearing flustered, Anita told him to move on before they were nabbed; 'We have plenty of time – the whole weekend,' she reminded him.

'It works out at only forty-seven hours until you fly away … that's not counting time for sleep.'

'And I need plenty of that,' Anita teased. 'Where are we going – or is it still a secret?'

'Heaven – a beautiful barrier reef at the north-east tip of the Florida coast, about forty minutes away. There are thirteen miles of soft sandy beaches for us to walk, a Victorian town with pubs and restaurants to feed your fancy, a museum to quell your historical curiosity and a 300-acre country club where you can pamper yourself in the spa, or sun yourself by any of the three beachside pools; and…'

'…all of this in one weekend? My, oh my.'

'…and, I was about to add, the annual Concours D'Elegance where some of the most exciting cars of the world are displayed for your pleasure.'

'It all sounds too much. My pleasure is in just being with you,' Anita told him; thus giving Alex the confirmation he was seeking. She felt as good as he did – well almost. As they speeded towards Amelia Island Alex told her about Jan, his agent, and her place on the plantation resort. He explained that she lived and worked mostly in New York but used the apartment, where they would stay, for weekends. This made their regular contact more social than merely for business.

He changed the subject as they turned east for the Buccaneer Trail, which curved through the network of tidal creeks and salt marshes surrounding the island. He described how they contained many varieties of herbaceous, salt-tolerant plants. Most of this area was covered with wheat coloured cordgrass that was either flattened by severe winds or stood erect against the twice daily tidal flow: giving protection to many small plants and marine organisms barely visible to the human eye.

'I hope I'm not boring you,' he said and once again abruptly changed the subject. 'Did I tell you how beautiful you are? I would love to feast my eyes on you, but I have to keep them on the road. Oh hell, what punishment!'

'It seemed to me that you were enjoying driving and entertaining at the same time. That should be enough for anyone', she said as they followed the signposts to the golf course. With a sideways glance she added, 'Let me tell you before we arrive, and you go into a huddle with Jan, that you are not too bad looking yourself for an elderly married man,' and giggled.

Alex held out his hand to help her from the car stepping back as an electric shock travelled up his arm. He carefully suppressed his feelings, and managed to answer in an equally jaunty fashion.

'That's where you are wrong. I'm a youngish separated man now.'

At that moment Jan appeared to welcome them and, as she led them to the lift, Anita commented in a quiet aside to Alex, 'how times change'. Nothing could be more true, as I have found in my research, he thought.

They were each given a most luxurious bedroom, joined by linked balconies overlooking the ocean, and wondered at this old-fashioned courtesy. Clothes were quickly hung or shovelled into drawers, hands were speedily washed in their separate en-suites, and they were soon back close together again leaning against the rail and commenting on their amazing proximity to the pool, ocean and golf course.

'If we have time before supper, what about a swim?' Anita suggested. 'I could wash away the travel dust and the pool looks gorgeous.'

'Good idea,' he replied. 'So do you ... and I can't wait to see your taste in swim-suits.'

'Cheeky ... seriously, I will just ask Jan if she has plans for this evening and then change.'

Jan told them that she was signed up for a tennis foursome in half an hour, and then she had booked a table for the six of them in The Grill at the Ritz-Carlton for dinner; so they had plenty of time for rest and recuperation. While he was pulling on his trunks Alex calculated that they would have at least an hour for a rest after they had relaxed in the pool. Somehow he was not feeling like taking a nap.

The pool was in the shape of a large pineapple with a jacuzzi and waterfall fanning from the top. The water was pleasantly cool, and there were few early evening swimmers, so they were able to dive in and swim lengths, alternating strokes, until satisfied. Alex made sure that he chose the left lane so that he could check on Anita as he turned his head to the right to breathe, and was delighted to see that she was a strong and elegant swimmer. Anita preferred breast-stroke and back-stroke to crawl so was able to watch the strong long legs just ahead and admire his powerful progress through the water. After a good work-out they climbed up the steps and stretched in silence side by side on two cushioned loungers; enjoying the last warmth of the setting sun.

'I like the way you move through the water, sweetie.' Alex told her. 'How about a drink?' He shrugged when Anita refused, wondering whether he was moving too quickly.

'Let's wait until we are changed and sitting on the balcony enjoying the evening shadows,' she suggested.

Wrapped in the pale blue towelling robes they had found hooked on their bathroom doors they walked back to the apartment, with hands joined, and made for their separate showers. Not for long. The warm power-shower was massaging her head and shoulders as Alex stepped in to join her. They stood under the deluge loosely holding each other, staring for a long moment through the rivulets of water on their faces. Neither knew how to cool their desire or whether they wanted to.

After they had gently kissed each other Anita stood back, away from the streams of water and ardour. Watching her every move, Alex said, 'I couldn't wait.'

'I know, but you will have to. We should wait until we are dry. After the swim I am as wrinkled as a prune and do not look or feel my best.' Alex reached for his towel, stepped out of the shower and, still looking at her, rubbed himself dry and shrugged into his towelling coat.

'We can't have that, can we,' he said. 'I am not expecting to be turned down a third time, however.'

Jan was an elegant and stimulating hostess as she worked to please everyone and oversee proceedings, and the dinner was a huge success. They were all dressed in their finery and enjoyed the lively conversation of a group of strangers who wanted to find out as much about each other as possible. Alex was asked to talk about his proposed book and found his ideas were very well received even though he was yet to decide on the story's finale. He listened attentively to several ideas, which were plausible. The couple from Jacksonville entertained them with golfing stories as they were involved in some way with the World Golf Village and had met many well-known PGA players. Jan's lawyer made up the party and was apparently an excellent tennis partner. He had recently had a half-knee operation, which had only improved his play and afforded them many jokes. Anita was the star of the group to Alex, however; he couldn't take his eyes off her as she turned her blonde head from side to side to talk or listen to each person in turn. He wanted to touch her but the table was too wide, and his wandering foot failed to make contact. Physical contact would have to wait.

Later, to save having to open and shut their bedroom doors and alert the hostess, Alex left his balcony door ajar and checked that Anita had done the same. So it was that sometime after midnight he walked through the gossamer drapes of her room and, to the light of the moon, slid into her King size bed. She was on her side, facing away from him her legs bent, and as he listened to her regular intake of breath and gentle sighing exhale he believed she was asleep. Once again he must wait. He kept quite still, lying on his back with his arms loose by his side, and shut his eyes. After a few minutes he felt drowsy and turned over towards her back slowly inching nearer until he was tucked close into her curves. Totally content, he fell into a deep slumber. He woke with a startled jump to hear her soft whispering in his ear, felt her hand stroking his face then her lips pressing against his. He pulled her gently on top, feeling her silky skin brushing against his chest, as he timed his breathing to fit with hers. She started to rock, gently at first and growing in strength until their two bodies moved as one to a distant drum – beating out the words: 'I love you, I need you, I want you.' Still joined, they turned over and Alex leaned back above her, on extended arms, looking into her wide-open eyes and waiting lips before plunging into her moist depths and moaning with pleasure as they melted together. 'This is the way it must always be,' he thought as they lay in each other's arms, eyes misty, their bodies glowing in the moonlight.

Never was there a more contented or cool couple than the one sitting on poolside chairs the next morning. Jan, dressed in white shorts and T-shirt, could detect their happiness from the smiling welcome she was given and was loathe to disturb them.

'What a wonderful day,' was Alex's greeting and Anita said, sighing, 'It's paradise.'

'It must be,' Jan said, handing Anita a bottle of sun spray, 'after the weather you have been having in Baltimore. I have been asked to play tennis again this morning so enjoy … do you two play tennis?' she asked.

Alex told her that he used to play regularly when he was young but had been too tied up lately. This was, he knew, a euphemism for 'depressed'. Anita said she also used to play but had not picked up her racquet for several years.

'Maybe we will both take up the game again … not this weekend, but in the future,' Alex suggested.

'It sounds to me as if you two will be 'taking up' a

number of things in the future. You will be very welcome houseguests whenever you can make it.'

Anita laughed and said how much she was enjoying this weekend and thanked Jan profusely.

'I will be back for a swim at eleven ... ish, then we must have a short session working with your draft... I have a few suggestions.' Jan told Alex and then set off for the red clay courts.

'Uh, uh ... it sounds as if the draft doesn't pass muster.'

'Nonsense, Alex. Have confidence ... after all, you can easily make any necessary alterations. At least you have some writing to adapt and a great story to develop,' Anita told him and rose to give him a long kiss. 'For the moment all we have to think about is the pool,' she added, scooping up a handful of water and throwing it at him, before diving in.

Before lunch, Jan and Alex sat in the shade of an umbrella and worked through the many changes that Jan's team of readers had suggested. Alex made notes of the pages where conversations were too long, too short, unnecessary, or not applicable. There were chapters that needed more substance and those that needed trimming. It was vital, Jan told him, to concentrate on the *Carina* story throughout. Jan was very upbeat and Alex was left with the feeling that she was pleased with his work, as they helped themselves to the poolside salad buffet. Over lunch Jan talked about deadlines. She had pencilled in the month of September for the book launch and visits to radio stations and bookshops and malls for signings. 'Was that convenient?' she asked.

'I should be back from Egypt by then,' Alex quipped, tongue in cheek.

'*Egypt*?' exclaimed both the ladies in unison.

'Yes ... I meant to tell you both ... Jake and I will be returning to El Gouna to have *Carina* lifted out of the water and cleaned. I have decided to pay for a full survey to see if she is worth any further expenditure – or whether she should be left to sink to the bottom of the Red Sea.'

'Plan your critical path for the middle of the month then we will both have some leeway,' Jan said, adding by way of an incentive, 'I predict that the end of this year will be a busy time for us all; so enjoy the sun.'

They spent the afternoon at the car rally, amazed at the high standard of workmanship and care that had been lavished on the vintage vehicles, and had a quiet evening walking the town and enjoying a simple shrimp supper in a friendly waterfront café overlooking the river. They watched the sun setting over the marshes and the boats returning to their moorings after a day's fishing. Their chat was simple too; the sort of affectionate banter that new lovers enjoy. Both refrained from broaching any serious subject. They were enjoying being together too much to spoil the fun.

It was on the following morning as they walked the beach barefoot, carrying their sandals, that Anita asked the first serious question: 'I have my suspicions ... did you really have to drive all this way to discuss your book with Jan? Surely you could have dealt with any changes on the Internet?'

They both laughed and hugged each other. 'You're right,' Alex told her, 'I must admit it was an "arranged" weekend; an excuse to get to know you.'

'And it seems to have worked out fine,' said Anita, 'I can hardly stop smiling.'

'Ditto, as Rush Limbaugh would say.' Alex joked.

Twelve

As he drove carefully back through the marshes Alex was mindful of how much he hated the idea of watching Anita fly away, after such a short break. Whilst they both felt that they had always known each other, there were aspects of their lives still to be explored. Alex wanted to know whether she was involved with anyone else and Anita would have loved to ask him about the break-up of such a long marriage. They knew that they would have plenty of time to answer these questions when they met again. The problem was that neither looked forward to spending any time apart.

It was not until they were waiting in the departures lounge that Alex realized what he must share with her. He needed to tell her about his parents, knowing that she would understand. After all, as a prisoner, she had been through hell. She was not a spoilt or sheltered individual, who had only known the pleasant aspects of life. She would understand. So he told her the story, his head down so as to avoid eye contact. As he quickly described the horrors, he watched the tears splash on his large gripped hands, and was shocked by the intensity of his emotions.

'I believe that psychologists call this the "hand on the door" syndrome,' she said after he had calmed himself. 'Often, when a patient has something really relevant to talk to them about he, or she, discusses everything that comes to mind – not the real reason for their visit – only to introduce the subject just as they are leaving. I know that I am the one to be leaving … but you know what I mean.'

'You're right … this is not the time or the place … please forgive me.'

'My love, there is nothing to forgive. I am delighted that you have confided in me and believe that it will help us to understand each other better. Hey – that's too formal – just say I will always be ready to listen to anything you have to tell me.'

'Same here,' was all he could say as the flight was announced, and the passengers for her flight crowded towards the last ticket check. After an urgent embrace she was gone.

For the following months they kept their promise to listen, using every possible time and method to communicate their love and loneliness. It would be with some misgivings that Alex set out with his son for the second trip to Egypt; they would be so far apart.

Once home, Alex attempted to find a time when he and Mary could talk calmly and quietly about their situation. This was not easy; when she was not at work or visiting her mother or friends Mary seemed to be either out walking or jogging or shopping. The time she did spend at home was when Jake was around and they were all preparing, eating or clearing away their meals. After over a week he at last caught her with time to sit down and share a bottle of wine.

'The first item on my agenda,' he told her, 'is this ridiculous idea that I should move out. This was my parents' house where I grew up, and whilst you have made it into a comfortable home, it would be unjust of you to claim it for yourself, your friend and Jake. If you want to lead separate lives then that is possible. The house is large enough for us to keep to certain areas and not intrude on each others' privacy. I can move into the guest room if you like.'

'That would be a good idea,' she told him. 'We no longer keep the same hours, and this would enable me to come and go as I please. This would preclude having anyone else to share the housekeeping costs, however, so we will have to split those between us; and the food bills and the savings account for Jake's college costs. How does that sound?'

'Fine. Let's see how we make out. You will have a chance to find out if your friend is easier to live with than I am; and if she does come up with her share of the costs. I will be away for most of the summer vacation and Jake would like to accompany me. We plan to revisit Egypt.'

'Hold on a minute ... he hasn't mentioned this to me. What on earth is the point of going in the middle of the summer ... we decided that it was far too hot.'

'We won't be staying in Egypt for very long as we intend to do some travelling in Europe. It is a good time for Jake to visit some of the countries he has read about and try out his French.'

'I see. It seems that this is something we could have done as a family if you had ever earned enough to save for expensive holidays.'

'That's true, but I have recently collected back payments for some of my work and I have a newfound taste for travel; a good thing for both of us.'

With that Mary stood and left the room in a huff, slamming the sitting room door.

Alex wandered into his office to send an e-mail to the agent in El Gouna:

'Please arrange for the yard to tow *Carina* from her mooring and lift her out of the water for a full survey, at my expense. Please also arrange for the surveyor you suggested to send me a quotation for undertaking the work. I will be staying in El Gouna mid June and I hope to be able to do business with you then. Thank you, Alex Johnson.'

A response arrived an hour later:

'Mr Johnson – we have made arrangements according to your instructions. Will let you know the dates for the work. Looking forward to seeing you again. El Nautico Agency.'

After a two-day journey Alex was to find that no such arrangements had been made. When he asked why *Carina* had not been lifted out of the water, he was told that there was a queue of boats to be dealt with before theirs.

'But we have been booked for two months,' Alex told them in an irritated voice. 'I thought that the survey, which I agreed, would have been done by now. Will you come to the yard with me to make sure that we are the next in line?'

'You see, sir … no one has been paid. It is the history of the boat. They all know that big sums have never been settled by owners,' Ahmed told him '…and how do I know you will pay my commission? For years I have been taking sheikhs, dictators, drug barons and others to see the boat. No one has ever been interested. Why should I help? That is not my job.'

'OK, come with me to the bank.' said Alex, 'I will organize a money draft for you and the yard. The bank will hold it until the work is done. How does that suit you?'

The agent rose from his chair, grumbling. 'You will need cash for the workmen. They will not haul without.'

'And I have no bundle of cash on me; you know the currency problems here.'

'Then leave me your Rolex and I will cover that side of it, until you have been to the bank,' the agent suggested. Reluctantly, Alex slid the watch from his wrist and handed it over.

'This was a special present. Please take care of it for me,' Alex said, watching as Ahmed opened his safe and placed the watch inside, turning to say, 'You will have it returned, when everyone is paid,' he promised.

When Jake, who had been swimming, heard about the watch he said, 'presents can come in useful, Dad. Can I ask who gave you the Rolex?' Alex did not answer. They arrived at the dock to find two or three small boats tied on the pontoon waiting to be lifted out of the water but nobody working. The agent had a heated discussion with the workmen and then approached Alex with, 'they say it is too hot. They need to rest until the sun sinks lower.'

'And when will that be?'

'They say about three o'clock.'

'Have they agreed to lift *Carina* next?'

'Yes, but it will cost more dollars,' the agent replied, rubbing his hands together.

Jake muttered something about bribery, and Ahmed offered to take them to lunch as he had once promised.

'Thank you, but Jake and I will walk to that café over there and be back here to meet you at three,' Alex told him. 'Please don't be late; we must make sure she is lifted today. I rang the surveyor and he will be here at ten tomorrow.'

At three o'clock precisely Jake and Alex walked back to the yard to find the workmen manoeuvring *Carina* into the dock. They secured the three wide strops under the yacht and connected them to the high lift. The foreman pushed a button and slowly the boat rose out of the water. When she was clear the high lift was driven to the boat park where she was lowered onto a cradle, and a ladder was propped up against her hull. The agent was smiling when he approached.

'You see … not too difficult. I will be here at eleven tomorrow to talk to the surveyor with you.'

'Make it ten. You may have to ring him to find out where he is.'

'I have other work to do, you know...'

Jake said, 'Bring your son. From the photos in your office he is around my age. Maybe we can be friends. He could visit us in the States?'

The agent reluctantly agreed, but said his son, Tedi, was away. Maybe they could meet another time. He explained that Tedi was a boat mechanic and was on the water, testing a reconditioned engine.

The following day the three of them were early and stood in the shade of the shed looking at the huge hull of *Carina* when an old man arrived, carrying his box of equipment. He wore large old-fashioned hearing aids (which whistled) and spoke with an English accent when introduced and kept repeating himself.

'Good day Mr Johnson, I'm hard of hearing, I say hard of hearing. I'm told you would like me to check everything and give you a verbal report – is that correct? I knew the owner well, poor man, I say, poor man. He had a larger more modern yacht, much larger than this one, which I surveyed. Never could understand why he bought this old German relic, relic.'

'Since you appear to have a poor opinion of the boat, I trust you will give us a true report on her condition?'

'What was that? Fair report ... of course, that is my job. Come back in two hours and I should be finished ... I say should be finished.'

After agreeing Alex and Jake walked into town, leaving the surveyor and agent with the yard manager, talking confidentially. When they returned the surveyor was just packing his equipment away in his well-worn box. He handed Alex a brief written report, which had been badly typed in the yard office:

'Fibreglass sheathing – no osmosis. Decks – sound.

Railings need replacing in places. Cabins – brightwork needs revarnishing. Hull – steel frames sound. Double-diagonal timber sound. Machinery – main engine and two side engines – appear to be in good order. Suggest injectors are recalibrated. Shafts – replace stern glands. Propellers – remove, clean, rebalance and replace. Generator – serviceable, should be replaced when possible with modern unit. Steering – hydraulics checked and found in good order. Throttle and gear controls – need servicing, excess play detected. Rot problems in the wheelhouse roof. Lighting – old but serviceable. Windlass – needs replacing. An elderly but well-found yacht with many years' life still in her. Signed Willy McIllium.'

'It looks to me that you have given her a clean bill of health, Willy.'

'I have had to give her a good report – she is sound, sound. Except for in the wheelhouse; I will show you, show you.'

They all clambered up the ladder, onto the boat's sandy deck, and entered the wheelhouse. Willy took a knife from his pocket and reached, with difficulty, above his head. There was a circle of small holes in the ceiling. He jabbed at the circle and one side of the ceiling collapsed. They jumped aside.

'You see . . . rotten! Needs replacing; I repeat . . . replacing.'

Alex thanked him for his thorough work and offered to help him back down the ladder.

'I'm fine . . . used to it, used to it,' Willy repeated, as he departed with a final long whistle from his hearing aids. Alex and Jake concealed their laughter, but soon had the smiles wiped from their faces.

'I have to tell you now,' said the agent, 'I have a deposit from the sheikh I told you about. He is buying the yacht and having the necessary work done in this yard.'

Alex exploded. 'Why you double-crossing son of a bitch!

Am I supposed to pay for the survey for your sheikh? Why didn't you tell me yesterday? I will come with you now to collect my watch, and you can charge the buyer for the yard work and survey – it's not my responsibility.'

As they walked to the agency, Jake and Alex talked angrily about the situation. It was obvious that the sheikh had promised to buy *Carina* only if the survey was satisfactory. They had been duped.

'I have an idea,' Jake said. 'Why don't we arrange to meet this sheikh? He may have his reasons.'

The agent was on the phone as they walked into his office, but quickly replaced the receiver.

'Here is your watch, Mr Johnson,' he said. 'I have talked to the buyer and he will pay the bills.'

'Whew. So this was a wasted journey for us. Will he also pay our fares?' Alex asked, but Ahmed merely shrugged.

'Can you arrange for me to meet this sheik? Ring me later at the hotel.'

Anxious to seem accommodating, the agent agreed, and the two Americans abruptly left the office.

A telephone call to their room, where they were basking under the turned-up air-conditioning, trying to make up their minds whether it was just too hot to swim, confirmed a meeting with sheikh Zayed: at six o'clock in the hotel lounge. They had worn straw hats with wide brims and smothered their faces and arms with sun cream but one look in the bathroom mirror told a sorry tale. Their faces were as red as ripe tomatoes. This climate was just unbearably hot. They had found themselves dehydrated after the short walk back to the hotel. The waves of heat rising from the baked pathway had felt like fire searing their eyebrows and the hair in their nostrils.

Much to his surprise, sheikh Zayed was dressed in

Western style with baggy striped cotton pants tied at his slim waist, and a loose white linen shirt. He was clean-shaven and had short dark curly hair. His sunglasses, with variable lenses, turned a pale yellow as he sat in the shaded room.

Alex was still trying to gauge his attitude when Zayed addressed him in a quiet tone. 'I hear that you were not pleased to learn of my proposed purchase of *Carina*.'

'I am very angry with the agent, not you,' Alex told him. 'Having arranged with him to have the survey I travelled from America to oversee the process. Now I find that you had already paid a deposit and agreed to purchase if the survey was satisfactory. Presumably you would have just walked away from the deal if not – leaving me holding the bills.'

'That is not as I see it,' he corrected. 'I did not know of the arrangements between you and the agent. Perhaps he was hoping for us both to pay the costs so that he could pocket the extra dollars.'

'Maybe,' said a thoughtful Alex. 'I expect you to take on all responsibility now. Let me change the subject … tell me what you are planning for *Carina*.'

'I was thinking of having her completely restored to her original condition, with a few up-to-date extras, and use her as an interesting venue for my models to show my latest designs. I am a fashion designer; I combine the old traditional styles and materials, local hand-woven silk and rayon, with modern trends. Do you like the concept?'

'An interesting idea. Where would she be moored?'

'The floating showroom could move from marina to marina, anywhere in the world, in keeping with the show timetables. Saudi to Milan, Monaco, Nice, Barcelona, Valencia or London; south to the Bahamas or west to New York; wherever the rich moor their yachts. A good skipper and crew would have a year to do the tour and I would fly to the nearest airports in my Gulfstream Five.'

'Would you have the restoration completed here? I do not believe they have the necessary expertise or equipment.'

'No. I am in the process of inviting various yards to quote for the work, but I have shipping friends who advise me that Gibraltar is one of the best yards in the world. Their workforce has many years of experience, the climate is perfect year round, they have all the necessary facilities in place and urgent supplies can be flown in to the nearby airport at short notice. The main problem I have is how to get the yacht through the Mediterranean to the Rock.'

'Can you have the engines serviced here, and the necessary safety measures dealt with, in order to sail her to Gibraltar yourself?' Alex asked.

'Those are my thoughts … exactly,' Zayed replied. 'The weather is good at this time of year for such a trip.'

Their conversation moved away from the boat for a few minutes as Alex was asked about his life in Florida and his family. He found himself relating some of the details of the Lavender Cottage Fire and hastily changed the subject back to *Carina*. The sheikh asked what interest Alex had in *Carina*; had he been planning to purchase her himself?

'To tell you the truth,' Alex confessed, 'I had not reached that decision. I have been researching the history of the boat and her nefarious owners for a book, and had wondered if I could afford to take her back to Florida to use as a home. Now that dream has dissolved I am only keen to follow what happens next; then I will write the end to this saga.'

'It seems to me, as a way of showing my regret for your inconvenience, it would be an idea if you were to take part in the voyage. Would that interest you, Mr Johnson? I must tell you that my own grandparents were killed in a similar fashion to your parents. An enemy tribe set fire to my grandfather's tented encampment and only a few of my relatives were able to escape. I understand your deep sorrow.'

'I would love to join the yacht ... but I am with my son who needs to return to the States at the end of September for school. Would there be room for the two of us? He could fly home from Gibraltar, I suppose, but we have a month to fill while the yacht is being prepared.'

'I have a house in Sardinia where I will be spending a month with my own family. There is a cottage in the grounds for guests. Would you and your son like to spend the time exploring the island? There is room on my plane if you would be kind enough to join me. I have taken on a skipper to manage the work on *Carina* so we could fly back together when he tells me it is completed ... say in a month's time.'

'That offer sounds too good to be true. We had planned to explore France, but we are flexible,' Alex joked. 'I guess we could easily change that to an Italian island renowned for its world sailing regatta. Opportunities like this do not come my way very often. I will have to ring my wife to tell her ... but she shouldn't have any objections.'

The sheikh laughed. 'The Costa Smeralda was discovered by the Aga Kahn in the sixties and has been developed by top Italian architects into a luxurious tourist destination. Near to our home white sandy beaches line beautiful aquamarine bays, and we overlook the Pervero golf club. We have a sizeable pool. The many VIPs who live or holiday on this stunning island enjoy luxury hotels and restaurants and a lively nightlife. How could your wife possibly object?'

'She will know that such a life style is way beyond my budget,' Alex told him, 'but maybe Alex could caddy at the Golf Club and I am anxious to pay my way if there is anything I can do for you.'

'Mr Johnson ... Alex. If you and your boy are to be my guests, you will not have to look for anything. I am, as they say, oil rich. My family and I have visitors from many countries. You will have time to make progress with your writing.'

Jake tried hard to conceal his excitement when he heard of the new plans, and immediately rang his mother to tell her the more incredible details. Mary was unusually offhand with him.

'Wow, that was difficult,' he told his father as he returned the receiver to the wall above his bed. 'I think she may be jealous...'

'Did she give you the go ahead?'

'I suppose so. I didn't really listen to all the "ifs and buts". After all, there is little she can do to stop us.'

So began the summer of a lifetime for both Jake and his father. The following evening they joined Zayed on the two-hour flight to Olbia Airport. He sat with the pilot in the cockpit and they were served with drinks and a snack by Cala, a lively hostess/secretary, who regaled them with amusing stories of her travels with the sheikh and his entourage. She hinted, confidentially, that he had three wives and they would all be staying with their children in Sardinia. Jake wondered if she had been primed to tell them this to prevent any future embarrassment.

On arrival they were met by a minibus and driven at speed through the hilly terrain overlooking the Costa Smeralda. The driver hooted as they turned in to a long drive, lined with olive trees, and the seven-foot high iron gates slid open to allow them through. Subtle floodlights illuminated the sprawling stone villa with its rustic tiled roofs fanning out in all directions, propped on rangy beams. The house stood on rising ground with the golf course and bay beyond. Cala showed them to a three-roomed annex, at the pool end of the house, equipped with every comfort, including a fully stocked cool box.

'Settle into your rooms,' she suggested, 'and tomorrow I will show you round the estate and organize transport for you. I believe there is a Volvo in the barn, which is for guests. Take a swim if you like.'

Once they had thanked her and she had left, with a friendly wave, they sat on their small terrace enjoying the cool air and scent of jacaranda; talking quietly about their good luck. At the far end of the pool was a high rocky promontory, on which had been built a large-roofed terrace overlooking a fairway, where the sheikh and his family were gathered to enjoy a meal. It seemed wise to wait until the morning for their swim. They may be honoured guests but obviously they were expected to care for themselves.

That was the way it was. By day they toured the island, visited the beaches, sailed in an old Laser, which Zayed kept at the Porto Rotondo Yacht Club, or swam. In the early evenings Jake reignited his father's interest in tennis or sat reading while Alex worked on his book. Some nights they visited the many first class hotels to sample their menus and night clubs; never once were they presented with the bill. On others they cooked a variety of fresh pasta dishes with market produce, which they found in a wicker basket on the kitchen table. Life was idyllic – not a worry in the world. That was until one evening, when they heard the sounds from the house of a bitter quarrel. Several men, who had been talking loudly, started shouting at each other in what sounded like Arabic. One called for them all to calm down – and they did for a while, but the angry shouting soon erupted again.

'Let's walk down to the golf club,' Alex hissed. 'Best if we are not known witnesses.'

Leaving the disruption behind they slipped through the pool gate and walked along the moonlit cart path by the course, towards the distant lights of the clubhouse. There they sat at the bar for a beer, and a chat about sailing with the Aussie barman. He recommended that they toured the island by sea – preferable to driving on the rough winding hilly roads – and suggested one of the week-long cruises. That was the only way to fully enjoy the crystal clear blue green waters around the coast with fish, soft fine sandy beaches and many inlets and caves to be explored. He was a professional yachting crewman waiting for the next regatta and, with no other customers, challenged them to a friendly game of pool in the clubroom before they walked back to the now peaceful villa.

Cala arrived the following morning carrying fresh bread and a bunch of grapes.

'Did you have a good evening?' she asked.

'Very,' Jake told her. 'I beat Dad at the pool table.'

'Oh good ... you were at the golf club. I looked in to ask if all was well, and found you gone. I have an invitation from the sheikh to join him this evening for dinner at eight.'

Alex thanked her, saying that they would be delighted, and asked what they should wear. Was it formal?

'Oh no. Just chinos and an open-neck shirt,' she told them. 'But be on time.'

At exactly eight o'clock Alex and Jake joined the sheikh's large family on the terrace. They were all dressed in cool flowing robes but spoke perfect English. The wives introduced themselves and their children, who ranged in age from five to thirteen, and the senior wife giggled as she told them that each of Zayed's wives was five years apart. The meal consisted of an anti-pasto delivered by young girls on large china platters filled with every conceivable delicacy. Then they had barbecued rosemary lamb with baby potatoes, onions and peas mixed in a mint sauce. Western food Alex thought but not strictly Italian … interesting. After a tray of cheeses had been passed around the table, one of the girls served each of them with baby hollowed-out pineapples filled with raspberries and served with creamy yoghurt. They all ate slowly and talked fast; sometimes many voices were raised at once.

Alex asked Zayed about his business ventures and found that these were many and various.

'I have a big problem at the moment with one of my concerns,' Zayed told him confidentially. 'That is something I wanted to talk to you about. It looks as if I will be unable to join you on the trip to Gibraltar. Will you two be happy to be in the care of my skipper and crew … and maybe help with the night watches … I know you are used to the sea.'

'Are you sure you wouldn't rather we flew home?' Alex asked him.

'Not at all. You will both be very useful for I have only my skipper, an engineer and another crew employed for this delivery. I would be very happy if you and your son would take the state cabin and play your part in life on *Carina*. I will arrange for my pilot to fly you back to Egypt when the time is right.'

There the conversation was closed and, after a suitable interval, the two men thanked their host profusely and said good night to each member of his family.

Thirteen

For the third time in four months Alex and Jake flew into Hurghada Airport. This time it was very different. Instead of a cramped seat in a scheduled airline they sat in cream leather extending seats in the sheikh's private jet, and the sheikh's air-conditioned chauffeur-driven Lincoln Town car replaced their small hot hired Volkswagen. Cala had been given the task, once again, of looking after the two Americans and drove them straight to the marina to see the yacht.

When they climbed on board they found the skipper, Pete, Tedi, the son of Ahmed and Hasina, Tedi's girlfriend, in the wheelhouse checking the navigational instruments. Pete introduced everyone and explained that Tedi was a trained engineer and could fix anything, and Hasina (which means 'good') was a great cook and would keep the yacht clean and organized.

'We must have a shakedown cruise to Hurghada and back next week before we set off for the Med,' the skipper told Alex. It seems that all the work suggested in the survey has been carried out, and I have arranged for sufficient provisions to be delivered to the dock once *Carina* is launched. Would you check the order and delivery invoices when they arrive please, Alex.'

'Certainly. I would like to study the charts with you, hear what course you have planned and how long it will take us. Jake has to leave for the States in six weeks from whichever airport is our nearest.'

'If the weather stays calm we should make Gibraltar by

the middle of August, allowing plenty of time for staging in ports for refuelling. I have the route mapped out on the electronic display. Come and see.'

He led Alex to the chart table and showed him the Mediterranean chart on the Transas Nav-Sailor. Each leg of their journey was clearly marked with distances and estimated times.

'After leaving Port Said at the top of the Suez Canal,' he told Alex, 'we have two long journeys. It is 400 miles to Crete and another 400 miles to Malta. For each we must allow just over fifty hours of sailing and we will plan to stop for two days at each island for refuelling and recharging our energy and food stocks. If all goes well, we then make for Tunis, which is 200 miles; the Balearic Islands, which are 350 miles; and Almeria on the Spanish coast. The final leg to Gibraltar – 150 miles – is the shortest but most congested waterway. Hundreds of cargo ships, tankers, cruise ships and long container ships all converge on the narrow opening between Spain and Morocco leading to the Atlantic Ocean.'

'How about fuel?' Alex asked. 'Fuel shortage was the problem on *Carina*'s last Mediterranean crossing.'

'*Carina* has a capacity of 2,000 litres, approximately 500 gallons. If we average eight knots we would cover 500 miles in sixty hours before needing to refuel. To be totally safe I have arranged for an auxiliary blister tank, to carry 150 extra gallons of diesel, to be placed in the library.'

'You seem to have covered everything in a short time in a yard that I had thought to be poorly equipped.' Alex told him. 'I am full of admiration.'

'Yes ... and that is despite the heat and limited daytime working hours. The men here are very experienced, and we were able to import all the equipment we needed within a couple of days. Good service.'

'What will we do about the port dues and refueling bills?'

'I have been given funds and a card to access them by the sheikh; with instructions to e-mail him if there are any problems. I will also pay the crew and all the provisions from this fund and keep account of all outgoings for him, on the laptop.'

Carina was launched early the next morning and they set off for the twenty-five miles along the Red Sea for a trial run to Hurghada and back. Hasina cooked a good breakfast and prepared a salad lunch while they were underway, telling them that the kitchen equipment was working perfectly. Tedi spent a couple of hours tinkering with the engines; checking on oil and fuel consumption. Alex, Jake and Pete were able to check the new Furino NavNet radar, Furino GP-320B GPS interfaced with their Brookes and Gatehouse autopilot and the Halcyon Fluxgate compass, which linked to the radar and autopilot. The crew all used the new Iridium Satphone to make brief calls to their families and friends to tell them their good news.

They made good time with a following wind and, after a walk ashore in Hurghada Marina to collect a parcel of linen, which had been delivered there for them, they returned to El Gouna before sundown. That evening they stowed their possessions and the boxes of tinned and frozen food and beverages, which arrived at nine o'clock. Then they talked through safety and radio procedures before turning in to their bunks. They planned to set off for the Suez Canal at crack of dawn.

It took them two days of cruising, with a hot, dusty southerly wind helping them along, to reach Suez at the south entrance of the canal. During this time they were able to work out their most economical speed and practise running on only one engine while Tedi topped up the lubricating oil. They had plenty of fresh food and were delighted with the imaginative international recipes Hasina could provide. At first, it was baking hot and they spent most of the daytime hours inside the wheelhouse. When on deck they took care to wear hats and plenty of sun protection. At night they ran the air-conditioning for five hours in order to catch some sleep. They knew that they would be eating tinned food and having disturbed nights on the long non-stop sections of the voyage.

Alex was astonished at the narrow width of the Suez Canal. There were only two passing bays before the central Great Bitter Lake, and two after. The rest of the 162 miles was only wide enough for one ship; but ship-to-shore communications along the route prevented any misunderstandings. They travelled beside the flat, deserted sandbanks at eight knots for twenty hours and were much relieved to see Port Said in the distance. Several huge ships were tied up to the quay, awaiting their turn to enter the canal. The skipper brought *Carina* alongside the concrete jetty; calling to his four crew to be quick with the warps. There was a strong headwind. Once safely secured, and carefully locked, they walked ashore to visit the pleasant city centre, with its flower filled borders and colonial buildings, and enjoy a cool drink at a local bar before setting off for Crete: on the longest passage of their journey.

At sea there were no strong winds or disturbed waves to impede their journey and they were able to maintain an average speed of almost ten knots. Day and night they kept a two-hour duty roster taking care to avoid the many vessels sailing towards the canal or away from it. The young couple took one watch, followed by Alex and Jake and then the skipper. This enabled each of the crew to see to their other duties and eat or sleep for four hours out of six. It was the custom for the present watch to be handed a snack and drink by their replacement. They worked well as a team and enjoyed each other's company, sharing tales of their very different worlds and adventures. Pete told them all about his home city of Halifax, the capital of Nova Scotia, and how he had worked on the tall ships in Lunenburg. He told Jake that his parents' home had been destroyed in a great storm and resultant fire just five years before and Jake told him all about the tragic fire that killed his grandparents in New Zealand.

An hour off the coast of Crete the sky darkened and a hot south-easterly wind started to whip up the sea. 'It looks as we are in for bad weather,' the skipper warned. 'This Scirocco wind warns of a low-pressure system ... look how the barometer is plunging ... we must be prepared for a rain storm.'

They made sure everything was stowed inside, and battened down outside, then speeded along the sheltered west coast of Crete. At the tip they changed course and travelled east, making for the safe Bay of Suda, and a mooring in the new marina in the port of Hania – just as the winds built to gale force.

'We were lucky there,' Jake commented to the skipper, as they were crossing warps to the jetty bollards to prevent surging as the swell entered the harbour. 'An hour later in sighting landfall and we would have experienced the brunt of those rising winds.'

'Yes, Lady Luck seems to be with us. All our new equipment is working well and *Carina* is making good time without using too much fuel. Using just two engines seems to be reasonably economical so we will only use the third for emergencies. Let's clean up and go ashore; I believe that Hania is a picturesque city with most of her old Venetian character preserved. Talking of that, I have been told that the fish is really great at the Venito Ristorante Italiano. Let's go folks.'

They passed lines of skeleton banana-shaped fishing boats backed up to quay, with their proud owners sitting chatting on the sea wall. Most wore white cotton caps hanging to their shoulders in points, which flapped like flags in the wind. Gentle drizzle grew to slanting sheets of warm rain, so they joined the fishermen as they ran for the nearest shelter, which just happened to be the restaurant.

A severe storm lasted throughout the night and the whole of the following day, so the skipper and his crew took the opportunity to catch up on some sleep before refuelling and visiting the market. After four days at sea they were used to the boat and taking turns with all the tasks. They were becoming accustomed to using the weather network and the single-sideband radio, and were in regular contact with their loved ones via the Internet; but relished being apart from the real world, enjoying the rhythm of the boat's demands – from sunrise to sunset.

This may be why, in their impatience to restart their journey, they left too soon. After the storm had abated, the sea was still in turmoil and took two days to settle. *Carina* headed out after only one day and it was rough enough to cause all the crew, except the skipper, to feel very seasick. They all took turns to reel down to the galley for hot drinks, returning quickly as the rolling below made them feel very poorly indeed. The following winds combined with the rolling seas caused the autopilot to groan as it moved the rudder to correct for the yacht's yaw. There were also one or two groans from her seasick crew. They had to reduce speed to lessen the impact of the waves, and took three days to reach Malta without any damage to the boat. As they motored towards Valletta they were all looking forward to a couple of quiet days.

During the trip Jake had been the fittest of the crew, hardly feeling more than a slightly dizzy head. He had read somewhere that seasickness could be prevented by standing square on two feet and studying the horizon; he found it worked. He was concerned about his father, however, and tried to help him by delivering dry biscuits and cold water to his cabin. He was also suspicious of Pete's behaviour. Up until now the skipper had seemed relaxed, and only smoked after a meal as he sat up on deck. Over the past two hours, although denying feeling ill, his features were sallow and sweaty and he was chain smoking in the wheelhouse; adding to the damp fug, which did not help anyone. He searched the horizon with his high-powered binoculars at regular intervals and repeatedly checked his bearings.

Sometime after six o'clock the seas calmed and the sky darkened. The boat speeded through the water in the growing gloom with the distant lights on the hillside of Valletta as their guide. Suddenly, Pete pulled back the throttles and told Jake that he was planning to stand off for a while.

'Is that a good idea?' Jake asked. 'Surely we should try to make for the marina before dark. It is so calm just now – maybe we are in the eye of a storm.'

'I am just giving everyone an hour to clean up before we enter the port,' he replied and left the wheelhouse and scanned the horizon once again through his binoculars.

Just then from the starboard side there was a wailing of horns and a blue strobe light whirled over their decks.

'We are coming alongside,' was the message spoken through an electronic hailer.

'Oh, shit!' Pete exclaimed. 'It's the bloody customs. Go and catch their warps, Jake.'

Once secure, four Customs Officers from the sixty-five foot aluminium Insure Patrol Craft jumped onto *Carina* – the last two with Alsatian dogs who were straining on their leashes.

'Who is the captain?' the senior officer asked. 'Please bring everyone to the saloon with their passports and I need to see all the ship's papers. Is the owner of the boat on board?'

'No, officer,' said the worried-looking skipper. 'I am in charge of a delivery from Suez to Gibraltar. We are just berthing here in Malta for two or three nights of rest.'

'We will be making a thorough search of the yacht. Please all stay here,' the assembled group was told.

For over an hour the men and dogs rummaged around in every corner of the boat. They used mirrors and strong torch beams to search the back of cupboards, sinks and lavatories and took no care with clothes, cases and their packaged presents. The crew talked quietly to each other; attempting to appear calm.

An excited barking from the dogs alarmed everyone, and Jake watched the skipper's terrified reaction as he was called through to the wheelhouse, and sternly asked for an explanation for something the dogs had discovered. During a calm patch, just after leaving Suez, the skipper had insisted they have a boat drill. He had timed their uncovering and launching of the fourteen-foot fibreglass Lund dingy from the yacht's davit, and they had all practised gently lowering down into the boat in their life-jackets. They had not touched the clearly-marked self-inflating black and orange Revere Offshore Ocean life raft, tied firmly to the foredeck.

All five members of the crew were now called to watch the unpacking of the raft's valise by customs. The officers swaggered round, displaying pistols at their hips, their yapping dogs stretching forward, ears alert, tongues hanging and eyes blazing. Their acute sense of smell had rooted out a stash of white powder; well protected from the weather in the vacuum-packed container. Twenty kilos in plastic bags were counted out and placed in a sports bag.

The crew was asked for their signatures as witnesses before being returned to the saloon for questioning.

Pete started with 'Let me explain…' but was told to wait.

'First I would like to know who you are, where you are from and where you are going. Let me start with the young lady…'

Each in turn answered these enquiries, and were asked to sign under their reports.

'Now can I explain?' the skipper asked. Pointing to each in turn he continued, 'This man and his son are American guests of the owner for the Mediterranean crossing. This young man is the ship's engineer I employed, and the young girl is his friend and our cook. I am the only person responsible for the running of the ship.'

'Thank you. We certainly have a problem. You had better tell me where the life raft came from, and whether you knew what it contained.'

'All the electronic equipment, the dingy with a Mercury engine, and the life raft were air freighted by the owner – I don't know where they were flown from – and delivered to me on the yacht one month ago. Here, I can show you the paperwork. The raft was sealed so I did not touch it.'

Jake now realised why he had been suspicious of the skipper. He knew instinctively that he was lying, and thought it probable that the trained customs men could hear the terror in Pete's tone.

'We will be keeping your passports for some time and impounding the boat,' they were told. 'When we are in port you must stay on board; your captain will be coming with us.'

Alex, still feeling weak from seasickness, had been very quiet during the whole scenario; recalling what he had heard about *Carina*'s arrival in Benghazi and the problems

Iraj and Sara had encountered with the Libyan police. He now spoke up: 'I believe there is an American Embassy on the island. Would it be possible to ring the ambassador to tell him of our plight?'

'In the morning I will bring the number and name for you. Now you must follow me into port and tie alongside our police jetty,' the senior man told him.

'Wait. When we are in port we will have to go ashore. We have no fresh food left and need to shop or visit a local café tonight. In addition we would all like to stretch our legs after encountering rough seas for several days,' Alex stressed in a firm voice.

The officer looked at him from under his beetle eyebrows and reluctantly agreed. 'You may spend an hour ashore with two of my men as guards. Do not speak to anybody while you are in Valletta. Do you understand?'

They just nodded their heads, and were relieved when the men and dogs returned to their cutter and set off. At full speed *Carina* followed in their wake, and after rounding the lighthouse on the harbour wall, found the customs men waiting on the customs dock. Having made fast and fetched his gear, Pete was bundled into a waiting van with a last look back at *Carina*, and the remaining four were almost frog-marched into town.

After supper Alex sent e-mails to Mary and Anita telling them of his problems and asking them both to get help in the States – it was only midday in Florida. The two guards watched like eagles from the wheelhouse as Alex then gathered his young crew together around the saloon table. He assured them that he was not in any way involved in this dangerous situation, and would do everything in his power to sort things out. Nothing could be done until the next day, so in the meantime they must attempt to get some sleep.

They had a very restless night and were woken at just

after seven by a loud knocking. Jake ran up the steps and stepped over the customs men to unlock the door.

'Hi, sorry to wake you,' said the young man, in a white, long-sleeved shirt and tie, who stood on the deck. 'I have come to collect you and take you to our Embassy building. Please pack up your possessions and follow me.'

He handed a notice to the two customs men who were far from alert and just grunted. They knew him.

'I am the Under Secretary at the Embassy – John Reynolds.'

'Oh great! I'm Jake … I will just fetch the others. Why not wait in the saloon while we throw our gear together. Thanks so much for coming to our aid so quickly. I won't be long.' And he rushed below.

It was a very bleary and tousled bunch that climbed into the Embassy car. Mr Reynolds informed them that they would be interviewed by both American and Maltese police officers, with a lawyer in attendance. He and the Ambassador were sure that there would be no problem. Their families had already confirmed their stories.

'The likelihood is, he added, that you will be on your way home by this time tomorrow.'

So their stay in Malta was short. After the interview they were given back their passports and tickets to London Heathrow; from where the young couple would take a flight to Cairo and Alex and Jake would make for Atlanta and home.

'Under some duress your skipper has admitted to knowing of the sheikh's cargo and will spend many years in jail', their lawyer told them. The sheikh would also be charged. The boat would be auctioned at the first opportunity. 'Not again!' Alex thought as he took the lawyer to one side for a private discussion.

Fourteen

The seas were lumpy and the dinghy slewed from side to side, pointing upwards then plummeting down on the next trough. Alex clung to the rope handles on each side but was losing strength ... the buzz of his office telephone woke him from this nightmare and he grabbed the receiver. He was shaken and in no state to take this call from the lawyer in Malta but managed to pull himself together.

'... Oh, yes ... thank you for letting me know. Next Saturday you say? I will try to be there. See you then ... bye.' *Carina* was to be auctioned in Malta the following month.

It had been a harrowing three weeks since he had returned from that island. First, he had found a note from Mary to say she would be away camping, not saying for how long. So he and Jake had been looking after themselves. Then he heard from Anita that she would not be able to meet him for a while, as her mother was ill in hospital. He had found it difficult to get down to writing his book as many intrusive questions and worries were destroying his concentration. He decided that his agent, Jan would give him some friendly advice after she had asked the inevitable questions.

'How did you get away with not being jailed?' she asked him after some preamble.

'I heard when I was home that Anita's mother had a great deal of influence. Her husband was some "high up" in the diplomatic service, you know.'

'You are lucky to know the right people, Alex. What will happen to your yacht now?'

'I heard today that she will be auctioned in the Malta marina next month and have been attempting to work out her true worth. If all the new equipment on board is included in the sale she must be worth over $70,000. However, there cannot be too many people interested in that old boat; there are so many modern fibreglass yachts which suit today's whizz-kids better.'

'Would you think of living on board yourself and gradually renovating where necessary?'

'That is a difficult question to answer as Mary is away and I need to find out what her plans are. Certainly the life afloat suits my character and I know Jake loves that idea.'

'In that case I would like to suggest that you go to the auction. I will give you a bank draft for $75,000 and we will both cross our fingers. If you are successful I will arrange with a ship-owner friend of mine to transport her back to Fort Lauderdale, as deck cargo.'

'What would I do without you, Jan? You will not regret this, you know. I may have to sell this home and split the proceeds with Mary, if we are to divorce. I can pay you back then. Would that suit you?'

'There's no hurry. Get yourself straightened out with your family and finish your book.'

'Thanks ... you are great,' Alex told her, and rang off before he became emotional.

So it was that on the 1st October, after a year of chasing *Carina*, Alex became her next proud owner. He had not been deterred by all the misfortune experienced by her previous owners, thinking only that he would be able to ensure a safe mooring for her in America. He was sure that Anita would enjoy lazy weekends on board. So the dreamer sat nervously at one the side of the marina shed, watching the excited crowd as the auctioneer started the sale. After a short history of Goëring's yacht and her many voyages he started the bidding. There were several bidders scattered in the crowd who waved their number boards. As the price rose there were only three to be seen. When the bids had reached $60,000 Alex only had one obvious competitor, who now nodded his head and dropped out. 'Done,' said the auctioneer, banging a hammer on an aluminium strut of the shed, and pointed at Alex, 'at $61,000 to the gentleman on the right. Thank you all.'

Alex took over a banker's draft and thanked the auction staff for their help. As he signed their paperwork they handed him a bunch of keys and wished him luck. He walked slowly through the many yachts on the boat park until he reached his own. He studied the name *Carina* newly painted on the stern, climbed the ladder and unlocked the wheelhouse door. Looking down into the saloon he found that the table and chairs had been pushed to one side: possibly to enable a potential buyer to view the engine room from above. He put the chairs to one side and rolled back the carpet. The table was difficult to slide so he gave it a tug and it tipped over, landing on his foot. Following a good deal of rubbing and cursing he had another try, pulling at the tabletop to lift it back on its feet. The top separated from the rusty screws, which had joined it to the undercarriage, revealing a hidden compartment. Nestling in the cavity was a brown paper parcel, which he carefully removed. He slowly prised off the seal, lifted the flap, and was astonished to find three small, frameless oil paintings, wrapped in tissue. Having resealed the packet with the utmost care, and emptied and dried his cool-box with a towel, he gently hid the packet inside.

* * *

After drinking the last cool beer, Alex took out his mobile and rang Anita's number; forgetting that for her it was only six o'clock in the morning

'So sorry to wake you, my love,' he said when he heard her sleepy voice.

'Alex ... is anything wrong?' she asked.

'This time I decided not to wait,' he replied. 'I have something very important to ask you. Will you marry me, when I am free?'

'Of course,' was her faint surprised reply.

'And I have something very special to show you when we are next together,' he added.

Now he had the perfect ending for his book.